CHILDREN of the FIRE

CHILDREN
of the FIRE

Harriette Gillem Robinet

Atheneum • 1991 • New York

Maxwell Macmillan Canada
Toronto

Maxwell Macmillan International
New York   Oxford   Singapore   Sydney

Atheneum
Macmillan Publishing Company
866 Third Avenue
New York, NY 10022

Maxwell Macmillan Canada, Inc.
1200 Eglinton Avenue East
Suite 200
Don Mills, Ontario M3C 3N1

First edition
Designed by Eliza Green
Printed in the United States of America

1 2 3 4 5 6 7 8 9 10

LIBRARY OF CONGRESS CATALOGING-IN-PUBLICATION DATA
Robinet, Harriette.
Children of the fire/by Harriette Gillem Robinet.
p.   cm.
Summary: A young black girl named Hallelujah lives through the
great Chicago fire with courage and resourcefulness.
ISBN 0-689-31655-0
[1. Fires—Illinois—Chicago—Fiction.   2. Chicago (Ill.)—
Fiction.   3. Afro-Americans—Fiction.]   I. Title.
PZ7.R553Ch   1991
[Fic]—dc20   91-9484

To Stephen, Philip, Rita, Jonathan,
Marsha, and Linda Robinet,
and to children around the world

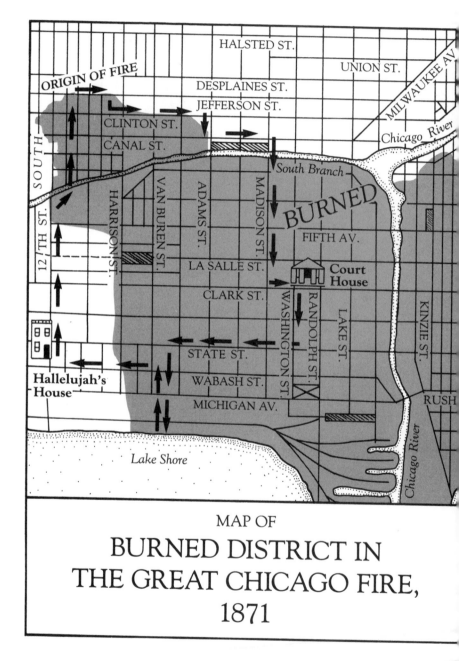

MAP OF

BURNED DISTRICT IN THE GREAT CHICAGO FIRE, 1871

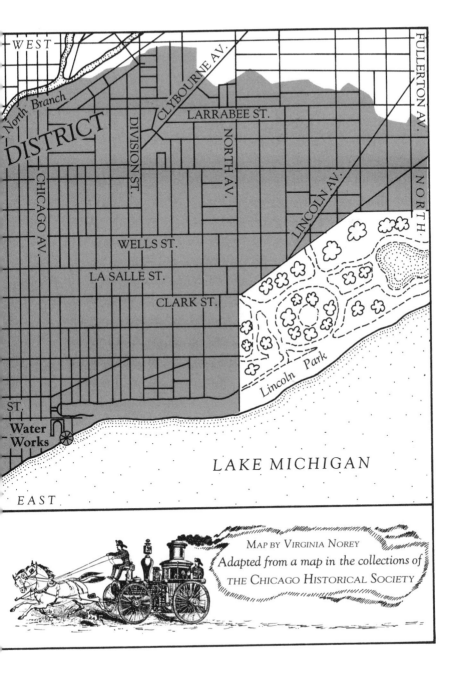

WEST

North Branch

DISTRICT

CLYBOURNE AV.

LARRABEE ST.

DIVISION ST.

NORTH AV.

CHICAGO AV.

LINCOLN AV.

FULLERTON AV.

NORTH

WELLS ST.

LA SALLE ST.

CLARK ST.

Lincoln Park

ST.
**Water
Works**

LAKE MICHIGAN

EAST

MAP BY VIRGINIA NOREY
Adapted from a map in the collections of
THE CHICAGO HISTORICAL SOCIETY

Chapter One

ON THAT SUNDAY IN 1871 A WARM WIND OFF
the Illinois prairie moaned. At times it howled, like spirits
of long ago, haunting the city of Chicago.

Dogs in the city tucked their tails, slicked back their ears,
and hid under porch chairs. Cats with fur raised along their
backs paced the streets, meowing.

Smoke in the air burned eyes and made tears trickle.
Chicago seemed to shimmer in a haze of smoke and fear.
The wind blew gritty dust that hissed like a deadly snake
against the kitchen door.

Inside the kitchen Miss Tilly wiped her eyes and stirred
the pot. She felt uneasy and worried about the recent fires.

Only young Hallelujah was not affected by the sense of
gloom that Sunday afternoon. She felt excited. She had a
secret plan to trick Miss Tilly.

"Why?" yelled Hallelujah. "Why?" Hands on hips she
faced Miss Tilly across the big kitchen.

Hallelujah was small for eleven. Her black hair hung in
six long braids that whipped around with her restless energy.
Her big black eyes burned like stars.

Miss Tilly wrung her hands. "Softly, softly, honey child. They'll hear you." She was brown of skin like Hallelujah, and wore her graying hair pulled back in a thick bun.

"Just tell me why?"

"Lord, give me strength," said the woman glancing heavenward as she sank weakly into a wooden rocker. The rocker was beside a black iron kitchen stove that burned wood for both warmth and cooking. On the whitewashed wall behind her a rifle rested on pegs.

"Now, child, you know the working men, both coloreds and immigrants, been having hard times. People laid off they jobs. You want we should let them hungry Irish right next door to us starve? It wouldn't be human, let 'lone Christian."

Of course Hallelujah knew this. Miss Tilly had explained it to her a dozen times before. And she didn't really want her friends or their parents to go hungry. Today, though, she planned to get something in return for carrying the food.

She stepped closer to Miss Tilly as a train whistle blew.

"Why me?" she asked, hammering a thumb against her bony chest. "Why not Edward Joseph? Why not Mary Jane? Why not you?"

Hallelujah's outrage was pretended because in truth she was delighted that it was her job to carry the heavy pot of good smelling boiled potatoes and cabbage. Two or three times a week she hugged a warm pot of food close against her unbleached cotton dress. It made her feel strong to be able to carry it.

Carefully she would take one step at a time out the kitchen door; then down the steps she'd go into the warm air of this strange autumn that was dry as white bones in the sun. Brittle leaves popped and crumbled under her feet as she crossed from her yard to the yard of the Sullivans.

"Child," said Miss Tilly with a sigh, "it's like this. Them Irish people don't feel so bad when a little colored girl brings over a pot of boiled cabbage. They be ashamed to take it from me. Or from your sister. Or from Edward Joseph. We be grown, you see. Them white people proud."

"Why do we pretend we aren't doing it?" Hallelujah was honestly curious about this. "Every time they see me coming, all the children run and hide. Then I leave the pot on their steps, and walk back. The women sneak out and take the food. The next night they leave the scrubbed empty pot on our steps." She lowered her voice. "And nobody ever says anything about how it tasted. And nobody thanks us. Mr. Patrick tips his cap and says, 'Evening's bright and beautiful, ain't it?' " She imitated his heavy Irish brogue. "But he don't say thanks."

"I told you, honey child," said Miss Tilly. "They proud. We offered them help, food, when we first knew Sullivan and his brother lost they jobs at the reaper factory. They said no. They can't take no charity. But they ain't so dumb as to starve. They accept a pot of ham and cabbage left on they steps." She shook her head. "I know it be hard to understand." She stared through white cotton curtains at the house next door. The wailing wind whipped her curtains and pelted the house with grit.

Hallelujah hated those curtains. It was always, "Take your dirty hands off the curtains, honey child."

Through the curtains Hallelujah saw the Sullivan house next door. That house and their own house on State Street and Twelfth were alike. They were part of a two-block tract of homes built right after the War Between the States.

The builders used lumber cut to lengths at a planing mill, and boasted that two men and a boy could raise a balloon-frame house in a day. Their home had cost $350. Paying $25 down, Miss Tilly and her husband, Mr. Joseph LaSalle, paid for it in the three years required by contract.

Hallelujah decided that Miss Tilly was daydreaming as she gazed out the window. Another train whistle blew. Their house was not far from the train tracks. To get Miss Tilly's attention back, Hallelujah banged an empty cooking pan.

"Beeswax!" she yelled. Then, imitating the preachers giving sermons on soapboxes in the park, she continued: "For once listen to me. Far away in Mississippi I was born into this world through no fault of my own. Now here I am the only child in this house in Chicago. I not only do all the child chores, but I do grown-up chores, too. I wash dishes a whole week at a time the same as Mary Jane. Sometimes I think I'm a child-work-worm!"

Miss Tilly shook her head sadly.

As Hallelujah gave her dramatic speech, she had waved a saucepan in one hand and a wooden fork in the other. But for every complaint, an inner voice answered her.

Her conscience told her that they always listened to her. And every job she did, though she hated to start, she loved by the time she finished. Besides, much of the time she managed to avoid work. Miss Tilly only asked for her help when she really needed it.

Hallelujah continued: "I can lug heavy pots of food all

right, but when it comes to letting me watch one of the fires around town, I'm too *young*." There, she'd said it.

"Now, child," whispered Miss Tilly, as if her whispering might lower Hallelujah's voice.

Just then Mr. Joseph pushed open the kitchen door.

Hallelujah's hands slid off her hips. She dealt with Mr. Joseph differently. Her fingers began to play with the skirt of her tan dress, a dress that reached her buttoned hightop shoes. Since Mr. Joseph owned a shoemaking business, she always had fine brown leather shoes. She loved how Mr. Joseph always smelled of good leather and shoe wax.

"Is there a problem in here?" asked Mr. Joseph in his deep voice. Tall and husky with cane in hand, he walked with a limp.

Hallelujah twitched her skirt coyly. With a sly smile she said: "Miss Tilly was thinking of letting me go watch the next fire."

Miss Tilly shook her head no, but her husband didn't see.

Mr. Joseph said, "So long as it ain't during no school hours. I don't want you leaving your lessons, now." He shook his finger in fatherly firmness.

"No, sir, Mr. Joseph," said Hallelujah. Holding her full skirt out at the sides, she curtsied sweetly to him. Now that she had what she wanted, permission to go to the next fire, she quickly started for the boiled dinner.

She knew she had been lucky, and she wasn't pushing her luck further. Meekly, she lifted the pot and started out the kitchen door. Behind her back there was furious silence.

She suspected Miss Tilly was shaking her fist at her husband. She suspected Mr. Joseph was waving his huge hands helplessly in the air to say he was sorry. She had tricked them again, but it made her feel sad, instead of happy. She was a morning child with the heaviness of evening in her heart.

To feel better, she tried humming as she crossed the yard. Jittery striped ground squirrels kicked up dry leaves as they raced into sandy burrows to escape. High in a cottonwood tree a blue bird called anxiously to his mate.

The air outside was warm and dry. An uneasy haze of gray, and the odor of sharp wood smoke, lent an air of doom to that Sunday afternoon. The wind rained dust from crumbled clay.

Hallelujah looked up at the October sky, bright blue in spite of the smoky haze. Wispy clouds blew rapidly across the sky like woolly white lambs running away. She paused to search anxiously for dark rain clouds, and grinned when she saw none. She thought it would be terrible for a big rain to stop the fires right then, just when she was going to go to the next one. So far, the dry summer and even drier autumn had made Chicago like kindling in a fireplace.

She left the good smelling food on the Sullivan back steps. No one was around, but she sensed hungry eyes watching her, sensed voices hushed at her presence.

When she reached home, she heard a loud argument. Edward Joseph, Miss Tilly's seventeen-year-old son, was saying, "A fire is no place for Hallelujah. She'll just get in the way of the fire fighters. She might even catch her skirt on fire."

"And you knows her. She'll be telling the firemen how to do they jobs. Lordy, Mr. Joseph, what have you done did?" Miss Tilly added.

"But the child said you wanted her to go," her husband said.

Through the screen door Hallelujah saw Edward Joseph fold his arms. "That girl gets her way about everything in this house. None of the rest of us do."

"Now, Edward Joseph," his mother said. "She's just a poor little orphan child. She can't hardly remember her own mama."

Orphan! Hallelujah hated that word.

Standing outside, she balled her fists and gritted her teeth. Being an orphan made her angry, made her sometimes act mean; and after she acted mean, she felt even angrier. The word orphan seemed to say that she wasn't as good as other children with living parents. It seemed to say that she was someone to be pitied.

Of course her sister Mary Jane was an orphan, too, but she was grown up. It didn't seem to bother her.

Inside the kitchen Miss Tilly raised her eyes to the ceiling. "Lord a'mighty, give me strength to raise this child rightly. Lordy, but it be hard! She worry the heart clean out of my body."

"She needs a spanking, that's what," muttered Edward Joseph as Hallelujah banged the screen door. She stamped her feet as she marched noisily through the kitchen, head high, hands switching her tan skirt from side to side.

"Don't go far," called Miss Tilly. "We be having supper soon as Mr. Post come home." Mr. Post roomed and boarded with them.

"I won't," Hallelujah called back, sour as a pickle.

She had planned to go out the front door, but she saw a horse and wagon pull up. She recognized Mr. Thomas

Baker, a short, muscular deacon at their church, who visited regularly to see how Hallelujah and Mary Jane were doing. He worked as a messenger for a bank.

This was the man who found them a place to live when Hallelujah arrived in Chicago with her mother and sister. Her runaway slave mother had walked from Mississippi north to Chicago to make her children free. Thanks to Mr. Baker, they moved in with the LaSalles, Mr. Joseph and Miss Tilly. After their mother died, Hallelujah and Mary Jane stayed with the LaSalles.

Hallelujah felt ashamed. She respected Mr. Baker, and today he would get a bad report on her again. She ducked her head and ran up the steps to hide in her room.

After a Sunday supper of baked ham, corn bread, boiled cabbage, and potatoes, Hallelujah sat on the front porch with the family.

Mr. Joseph, Mr. Post the roomer, and Edward Joseph were all lined up in straight chairs on the porch, and Miss Tilly, wearing her bonnet, sat in a rocker. The men were dressed in brown jackets and caps, and looked like nervous sparrows on a breaking twig.

Wearing a tan cotton bonnet to match her work dress, Hallelujah sat hunched on the top step. Back in the kitchen, her sister Mary Jane noisily washed dishes. Hallelujah felt gleeful that this was Mary Jane's week to do dishes.

The past week it had been Hallelujah's job. Sunday and Monday she had slowly washed dishes in the sink in sudsy water, and rinsed them in a pan of clear water, drying them with linen dish towels. Tuesday and Wednesday Edward

Joseph had washed dishes for her. He did it to keep her from telling that he had gambled part of his pay from the grain port. Thursday she managed to prick her finger. Tender-hearted Miss Tilly washed dishes for her that day.

Friday and Saturday Mary Jane washed dishes for Hallelujah. Her plump, pretty sister worked with Miss Tilly at Armour's Meat Packing Company in the North Division. Since she was only sixteen, Mary Jane handed her pay of four dollars a week over to Mr. Joseph.

However, unless Mary Jane washed dishes for her, Hallelujah threatened to tell that the pay had increased to four-fifty a week. Mary Jane was saving the extra fifty cents for herself. Shy Mary Jane had one interest in life, writing. She used the money to buy paper and ink for writing stories.

Hallelujah leaned against the porch railing and thought: I've been making Miss Tilly and Mr. Joseph do whatever I want; and threatening to be a telltale on Edward Joseph and Mary Jane. I'm a little stinker. A skunk! she decided.

Mr. Post cleared his throat. Short and fat, Mr. Post drove horses for a cab company. He dressed in brown suit and tie every day, and wore a brown bowler hat. A bachelor, he rented a room at the house and ate meals with the LaSalles. He said, "This is no night for a fire!"

Beeswax! thought Hallelujah. This is a *good* night for a fire. This would be *her* fire.

Chapter Two

"WIND'S STRONG ENOUGH TO BLOW YOU OFF the porch." Mr. Post crossed his leg then uncrossed it nervously.

Mr. Joseph answered, "Coming off the prairie." He leaned his ladder-back chair against the porch, and the chair squeaked. The squeak made Miss Tilly jump.

"Southwest wind," said Mr. Post, leaning forward.

They all watched as the lamplighter, ladder over his shoulder, stopped at each lamppost on the street. Opening the glass fixture, he lit their gaslight. They waved, and he waved back.

Edward Joseph leaned his chair back. "Lumber planing mill went up last night like tissue paper," he said. "Still smoldering this morning."

"You can smell the smoke," his father said, nodding.

"That the one on Canal Street?" asked Mr. Post.

"Between Jackson and VanBuren," Edward Joseph said. "Took sixteen hours to put it out. Them fire fighters are tired tonight and ready to sleep."

"Burned four blocks square," said his father.

Hallelujah grinned. The next fire was her adventure. She would get to see all the excitement. A gust of wind blew dirt in her mouth and eyes. "This awful wind," she said, spitting. "Beeswax!"

"Terrible," said Miss Tilly. "Blowing dirt and leaves in the kitchen every time I opens the door. Make work sweeping."

"Like I said," Mr. Post reminded them, "good thing that fire was last night. This is no night for a fire!"

The door at the Sullivans' slammed and Mr. Patrick Sullivan strode across the narrow yard. All the narrow front two-story houses were built one room and a hall wide, and four rooms deep on long lots. They were painted white, every one of them. The LaSalles' house was trimmed in sunny yellow. The Sullivans' house was trimmed in kelly green.

Patrick Sullivan was tall and muscular with a crop of red curly hair. "Evening's bright and beautiful, ain't it?" he said to his neighbors, but his low sad voice did not match his words.

When he saw Miss Tilly and Hallelujah, he tipped his cap politely. He sat on the top step across from Hallelujah.

"Good evening, Mr. Patrick," said Miss Tilly. "What's new?"

"Cyrus McCormick laid off more men at the reaper factory," he told them. "Ain't no jobs for working men nowhere in this city."

Mr. Joseph frowned for a second. Was Sullivan saying that because his shoemaking was a business, he didn't work? Workingmen and businessmen had this snobbery with each other, but did it matter? Shoemaking was falling off, too. Families out of jobs didn't buy shoes, or even get them repaired.

Hallelujah stared as Mr. Patrick drew on an empty pipe. "Why don't you fill your pipe, Mr. Patrick?" she asked. She knew children's questions always irritated him.

They were interrupted by a train loudly chugging into the station. Their homes were built between the Chicago and Northwestern, and the Chicago, Burlington, and Quincy railroads.

In 1871 Chicago was the center of the world's largest railroad network. That made Hallelujah proud to live in such an important city.

"It's them trains," Patrick Sullivan said. "Bringing more people into this town than can find jobs." He had ignored Hallelujah's question.

Immigrants from Europe landed at ports in New Orleans and rode trains north to Chicago. They landed in New York and rode trains west to Chicago. Mr. Patrick waved his pipe angrily toward the train. Then he pushed it back in his mouth and drew on it. He seemed to have forgotten that only a few years before, he had arrived on one of those same trains.

Hallelujah glared at the empty pipe. It irritated her. "Why don't you light your pipe, Mr. Sullivan?"

Mr. Joseph used his cane to nudge her in the ribs. Children were not supposed to talk that way to grown-ups.

She wiggled. Her bedtime was near. The sun had set behind the dry prairie like a dull burning ball in the west. Evening grew dark and frightening. Wood smoke in the air was sharp enough to make her eyes run tears.

Good judgment told her to stay silent, but curiosity itched her. Why didn't their neighbor fill and light his pipe?

She was kept from asking again by the sound of children

whispering. As smooth as oil she slipped down the steps and ran to join them. Maura, Daniel, and Patrick Sullivan, older children of the Sullivan brothers, each carried baskets.

"Where you going?" Hallelujah asked. They were allowed to leave home alone in the dark, and she was hardly allowed off the porch after sunset. It wasn't fair, she thought.

"Won't tell," said Daniel, who was seven and a redhead like his papa.

Maura was eleven, but head and shoulders taller than Hallelujah. She stepped protectively in front of her cousins. "Out," she answered.

Brown-haired Patrick was nine years old. He held a finger over his lips. Hugging their baskets, the three children ran away from Hallelujah.

"I know where you're going," she called softly after them. "You're going out to steal from the railroad tracks!"

She watched them with envy. How she wished Miss Tilly and Mr. Joseph needed her to pick up fuel. When clanging rail cars piled high with shiny black coal screeched into Chicago, clumps of coal often bounced off the cars. Poor children gathered this coal for their parents; coal to burn for cooking food, and coal to burn for warming the house.

Hallelujah knew something else the children stole, especially in cold weather. They ripped planks off the wooden sidewalks of Chicago at night. During the day, carpenters nailed new planks back onto those same wooden sidewalks. That meant the children provided wood for their families, and made work for the carpenters at the same time.

If police found grown-ups stealing sidewalk planks, they would lock them in jail. If they found children stealing the planks, they simply chased them away. The streets were also paved with wooden blocks, but they were harder to rip up.

Miss Tilly thought this stealing was a sinful shame. Hallelujah thought it must be wonderful adventure for the children. Why couldn't *she* have some adventure in her life?

Dragging her feet, she returned to sit on the porch steps. A rustling behind her warned her that Mr. Joseph was pulling his pocket watch out.

"It's long past the child's bedtime," he announced.

"My, my," Miss Tilly said with a sigh. "Such a warm evening. My mind be thinking it were summer. School tomorrow, Hallelujah. Go on up to bed, honey child."

Miss Tilly, like Hallelujah's own mother, Sophia, had fled slavery by the Underground Railroad to live in Chicago. She talked Southern slave talk. Mr. Joseph, on the other hand, was Chicago born and raised. He and Edward Joseph spoke like Chicagoans.

That Underground Railroad was not a train, however. Runaway slaves walked. Kind people known as "conductors" showed the slaves places to hide and rest. They found them food.

Sometimes runaways hid under hay on wagons for short rides, but for the most part, they walked north to freedom. After receiving food, they walked to the next "station" or resting place.

Bed! Hallelujah's back stiffened and she felt spiteful. "Maura, Daniel, and Patrick aren't in bed," she said.

Mr. Patrick almost broke his front teeth stuffing his unlit pipe in his mouth. By gaslight from the street she watched his face grow as ruddy from embarrassment as his carrot-colored hair.

She could feel the storm of Miss Tilly's silent shame.

Edward Joseph coughed. Mr. Joseph shuffled his feet in anger.

"Any child wanting to watch the next fire better go to bed," Mr. Joseph said sternly.

Quickly Hallelujah flitted inside. Mary Jane had finished the dishes, and was sitting in the parlor at the open window writing by the light of the street lamp.

Hallelujah found her hairbrush and comb and sat beside her sister. Mary Jane first stroked her hair lovingly, then unbraided her plaits. She combed Hallelujah's hair, jerking at the tangles. For the night, she braided it more loosely.

"I sure wish you'd be a good girl," she said softly to her little sister. "You clean tear the heart out of Miss Tilly and me."

After combing Hallelujah's hair, Mary Jane cuddled next to her and listened to the conversation on the porch. It was too dark now to write without lighting their own gaslight. From time to time Mary Jane poked Hallelujah, but the younger sister refused to go to bed.

Mr. Sullivan was saying, "I only made sixteen dollars a month during the war, but I could send it all to Mary Clare."

Both he and Mr. Joseph fought for the Union during the War Between the States. The war had been over for six years.

"I fought in the Twenty-ninth Colored Infantry for ten dollars a month. Got a hole in my leg to prove it." Mr. Joseph lifted his lame leg on his cane.

" 'Course," he added sourly, "they didn't allow coloreds to fight until the very end. First four years us colored men from Illinois fought with shovels rather than rifles." He laughed bitterly.

"Ten dollars? Are you sure?" Patrick Sullivan squirmed.

"Ten dollars if you were colored. You heard what he said." Mr. Post squeaked his ladder-back chair. "I'd have fought for *no* money to be a free man, but they wouldn't even take me in the Army. I tended horses during the war."

Patrick Sullivan's face flushed red again. Talk of slavery always embarrassed him. He turned toward the street. The gaslight flickered in the wind. An owl beat huge wings and swooped past searching for foolish mice.

At a sharp nudge from Mary Jane, Hallelujah stood and stretched. She made a quick trip to the outhouse in the backyard. Then she splashed water from the sink in the kitchen on her face and hands and rubbed them dry with a towel. She was about to go upstairs with a candle when the first clang of the fire bell rang. The men on the porch twitched and sat forward.

My fire! she thought. Jubilant, she snatched her bonnet off its peg in the hall and ran onto the porch.

"Probably some wood rekindled at the planing mill," said Mr. Joseph. He rubbed his chin nervously.

"Yeah. This one will be over fast," Edward Joseph said standing. Grinning, Hallelujah stood close by his elbow. He frowned at her and muttered under his breath.

Miss Tilly called, "Oh, Mary Jane. You wants to go along?"

"No, ma'am," Mary Jane said as she gathered her paper and pens to carry upstairs.

"We'll be back real soon," Edward Joseph promised, He grabbed Hallelujah's hand in a firm grip.

She hoped they wouldn't be back soon. This was her fire! It was 9:30 P.M. on the eighth of October, 1871, and she was hungry for adventure.

Chapter Three

EDWARD JOSEPH TOOK LONG-LEGGED STEPS
and dragged Hallelujah in angry jerks. They headed toward
the faint glow of fire.

"Now you ain't causing nobody no trouble at this fire,"
he said. "None, you hear? And the reason Mr. Patrick
didn't light his pipe was 'cause police been stopping smok-
ers. To avoid fires they can't smoke outdoors no more, you
hear?"

"Yes, Edward Joseph." She thought Mr. Patrick was rude
not to answer her himself, but he often ignored children.

"And besides that, you worry my poor mama's heart out.
She kept you and Mary Jane after your mama died. We
didn't have to do that. We could have sent you back to
Mississippi where you come from." He went on, "Mama
raising you like a little Christian lady. Keeping you in school
when she don't have to. Sending you to Sunday school.
When I was your age, I was working to help pay for things.
I wasn't no freeloader. But you, you wear taffeta dresses to
church. You and Mary Jane both. Looking like fine ladies."

Hallelujah thought: and Mary Jane pays for our dresses! My sister gives her pay to Mr. Joseph every Friday.

One reason she kept her mouth closed was that they were heading into gale winds. Dust and leaves blew in her face. Her eyes felt gritty. At the rate he was talking, Edward Joseph must have had a mouthful.

"If I was an orphan child like you," he continued, "I wouldn't sass a poor lady who took care of my dying mother. Who do you think you are anyway? Some rich child like them fine folks on Michigan Avenue?" he asked. "No, you ain't. You just a poor nigger. Your papa, he's dead. White man shot him for trying to escape slavery. You all alone. Your mama brought you up here to Chicago on bleeding feet, that's how. Running away from that same slave master. You just a nobody and making a fuss like you was somebody. You hear? You just a trashy little slave child!"

This opened that deep bleeding sore in Hallelujah's mind. Was she a nobody because she was an orphan? Did she have to feel grateful to the LaSalles for the rest of her days? Who was she anyway? Who was anybody?

She could take no more. She bit Edward Joseph's hand and snatched herself away from him. Under a streetlight he stared at his hand. "You draw blood on me? You little . . ."

Hallelujah's eyes were filled with tears, unusual for her. "You don't have to take care of me," she shouted. "None of you. I can take care of myself. I hate you. You ain't nobody. You just a . . . you just a . . . Chicago nigger, that's what! Leastwise we came *up* from slavery," she yelled. "You ain't gone nowhere. I hate all of you!"

She was aware that people hurrying along the street to

see the fire had gathered to watch their argument. That bothered her. It was none of their business.

By then they had crossed the railroad tracks and were going west toward a red glow in the dusty night air. It seemed the dull orange-red sun was rising again where it had set. Alarm bells from the courthouse began ringing again. This was now a general fire alarm, a big fire.

She couldn't stand to be jerked around by Edward Joseph any longer. She knew the city.

Chicago extended about three miles south, west, and north of where the Chicago River touched Lake Michigan. The river was shaped like the letter **Y** with a South Branch and a North Branch. The bottom of the **Y** touched the Lake. North of the **Y** was the North Division; south of the **Y** was the South Division. Land in the fork of the **Y** was known as the West Division. She could wander around on her own. She was fast coming to the West Division's homes of the poor.

She had been tripping along out of reach of her foster brother. From time to time Edward Joseph tried to grab her, but they were in a throng of people. He edged closer now, almost even.

Suddenly she turned and kicked him on the ankle, then dashed through a circle of working men, women, and children. She heard him howl and call after her, but she raced away. Quickly she melted into a crowd of other little girls in bonnets and unbleached cotton dresses. She was like a sunflower in a patch of sunflowers all bobbing in the light of the fire.

Walking behind tall grown-ups kept the wind out of her face.

Across the bridge over the South Branch of the Chicago River the glow grew brighter. It was brighter than two gaslights in a parlor. If she had her history book right now, she could have read the print, it was so bright.

Since she was a little fearful of the dark, she was grateful for the brightness. She missed holding Edward Joseph's hand, but curiosity pulled her forward. Most of the city she knew, but the West Division was not familiar. Once Mr. Post had let her ride with him on a Saturday when his horse-drawn livery cab delivered goods to the West division, so at least she knew the pattern of streets was the same square grid for all Chicago.

Someone bumped her elbow. "Ain't you gots no doll?" asked a thin girl her size. Hallelujah had never seen so many brown freckles on one white face.

"Why'd I need a doll at a fire?"

"I gots a doll, see?"

Hallelujah was about to say that the thing the girl was holding was not a doll, but she checked herself. The girl wore raggedy clothes, had dirt smeared across her freckles, and had a charming sweet smile.

"What's your doll's name?" asked Hallelujah. The doll held out was a mere corncob wrapped in print cloth from a flour bag. In spite of this, the doll made Hallelujah feel lonesome for her own special wooden doll, Suzy Dollperson.

The girl answered, "Betsy. What's your'n?"

"Suzy. She's home. Across the river and railroad tracks." She pointed behind her where the sky had picked up the red glow. But the dusty windstorm blew in front of them off the prairie, howling like Indian ghosts seeking revenge.

She remembered Mr. Post saying: "Good thing that fire was last night. This is no night for a fire!"

"Want to hold my doll?" asked the girl.

"No. Well, maybe a little while." Hallelujah didn't want to hurt her feelings. After all, she was a companion at the fire and Hallelujah had felt lonely.

The girl handed over the corncob doll as tenderly as if it were the infant crown princess of England.

Hallelujah nodded. "She's a . . . she's a . . . doll." She couldn't help wrinkling her nose.

"My mama's got a baby. Has your mama got a baby?"

"No," Hallelujah said. Should she tell the girl her mother was dead? She decided not to. But they were missing the fire. She grabbed her new friend's hand. "Want to run down this street and see if we can get to the fire before these people?"

The girl didn't hesitate. "I live on DeKoven Street. You know DeKoven Street?"

"No."

"That's where the fire started. Barn back of O'Leary house."

"Oh. You've been to the fire then."

"Yeah. Our home is on the same side. Wind blew the fire away from us. But my papa gots buckets wetting down the house just the same."

Hallelujah stared at her with envy. Now this was someone who was free. She could wander alone in crowds and have adventures. "What's your name?" she asked.

"Rachael. And yours?"

"Hallelujah."

"That ain't no person's name."

"Beeswax! It is," Hallelujah yelled. She shoved the doll back at Rachael.

Rachel stared at her. She adjusted the doll on her shoulder as if it were an infant in need of comfort.

"Ain't you Christian?" Hallelujah yelled.

The girl shook her head, no.

Hallelujah calmed down. "That's all right, then. That's a thing about Chicago different from the South. My sister Mary Jane says we're lucky to know all kinds of people here. I got Jews like you at my school. She got Jews at her work. And Teutons—that's what they call those Germans—and Irish, and Norwegians. Polish and Swedish and Slovaks, even."

"My folks from Poland, but I'm American."

"Me, too. When folks say bad things about immigrants and Jews and Catholics, well, I know it ain't true." Hallelujah sighed. "Now, seeing you ain't Christian, I'll tell you."

They stopped for a moment in the shadow of a huge oak. Low wooden shanties on the street were surrounded by pigsties and henhouses and stinky cow stables and corncribs and sheds. There was hardly space for two children to pass between the dry wooden buildings. The smell of animals was strong. Not like the sweet hay aroma of Mr. Post's stables or their barn.

Hallelujah glanced up and down the street. They were out of the wind, but she could see flames behind the silhouette of the dark houses. The windy fire seemed to be leaping and dancing like gypsies at a campsite. This was fun.

Rachael was staring, too. "Let's go see," Hallelujah said. They trotted down the middle of the dusty street.

"Anyway," said Hallelujah back to her name, "you know your Passover?"

Rachael stared at her. "Sure."

"Well, we have Easter then. And they say I was born into this world on Easter Sunday morning at sunrise. And my papa, he's dead now, he said, 'Hallelujah is her name.' "

"Angels sing Hallelujah. Means praise God."

"Yes." All those years and Hallelujah never knew that. It made her feel better. Rachael understood after all. Angels, eh?

They crossed Jefferson Street and glanced back. The fire was a massive yellow brightness that had burned a square block of shanties and sheds. Low flames licked up the wooden crumbs behind them like mice creeping out after supper.

Ahead of them the wind fanned flames like a yellow fire-breathing monster. It was leaping toward the sky and gobbling up more dry wooden shanties. Hallelujah fumbled for Rachael's hand. Rachael put Betsy in her other arm, and they squeezed hands.

We're both little girls, Hallelujah thought. She's not trash for being raggedy, and neither am I for being an orphan.

"All them folks' homes," said Rachael sadly. She sighed.

Hallelujah said nothing. She was thinking that all the junky wooden sheds and smelly cow barns and shanties were better burned down. Maybe they would stink less.

Men in overalls strode past them. One said: "Broad street." Other men wore nightshirts and pantaloons.

"Yeah," answered another man, "soon as it reaches a broad street, the fire will have to stop."

Boys ran past. "Any fire trucks yet?" they called.

"Fire fighters slow tonight. Must be tired," a man answered.

The girls walked more quickly. Rachael told her, "Ewing Street is a broad street. Let's go watch the fire go out."

Disappointment dampened Hallelujah's feelings. No firemen to watch and the fire might go out soon. "Beeswax!" she said.

She glanced behind her. Where they had stood under the huge oak was ablaze. Not little separate fires, but a shiny yellow ball of filled-in fire. She shook Rachael's arm and pointed.

"Uh-oh," Rachael said. "All them were running to the fire on my street. They don't know their houses are gone."

"It must have jumped over the . . ." Hallelujah stared. The fire was racing in the wind, but there was no black smoke; there was no fire smell. The wind carried smoke over their heads.

How could it be that way?

Walking now with their backs to the wind, they arrived at a burning street. On both sides of the street every house was in flames, but it wasn't hot. The wind carried the heat away. In fact, it was pleasant to be holding Rachael's hand and strolling down the brightly lit street.

Only the noise bothered Hallelujah. "Beeswax!" She held her ears. The wind howled and the fire was deafening, like twenty trains arriving all at once.

Rachael pointed. "Ewing Street."

Somewhat broader than other streets, Ewing had raised wooden sidewalks like downtown Chicago. Crowds of dazed-looking people wandered in the bright firelight.

Men in caps wore overalls or trousers with suspenders.

Women in bonnets or night caps wore mended dresses of unbleached cotton. Some women had no better than dresses of floursack cloth. Children wore torn dresses like Rachael or tattered pants. They were mostly barefoot. Some people who hadn't had time to get dressed were in nightgowns or underwear.

"Hey, Rachael," called a barefoot boy. His brown pants were torn at both knees and he carried a squealing pink pig under one arm. "Your mama's looking for you."

Rachael hugged her Betsy doll and pointed with her other hand. "Go see your house burned down."

The boy looked startled and ran away. Hallelujah felt sorry for him. Those shanties really did belong to people.

At the sight ahead of them, Rachael grabbed for Hallelujah's hand and squeezed until it was numb.

Before them Ewing Street suddenly crackled alive with flames. Fire licked at the dry sidewalks of raised wooden planks. All at once every house was burning.

The girls held hands and turned slowly in a big circle.

It was the most wonderful sight Hallelujah had ever seen, but a loud wailing cry went up from the crowd.

"Well, that man was wrong," Hallelujah shouted to her new friend. "A broad street didn't stop it."

Chapter Four

HALLELUJAH COULDN'T HELP FEELING PLEASED.
By no means was she sleepy yet, and her fire was turning
out to be a dandy. The boy had said that Rachael's mother
was looking for her, but Hallelujah hoped Rachael would
stay. She wanted company at the fire.

Rachael seemed dazed. "Where's my Betsy doll?" She
hugged her doll. "Here she is."

Quickly Hallelujah glanced at her friend. Rachael seemed
confused and worried; her eyes had tears welling up.

Rachael whispered, "All it was was Patrick O'Leary's
barn. That's all. What's wrong with this fire?"

She turned to Hallelujah. "I saw the warehouse. Did you
see the warehouse fire?"

Hallelujah hated to lie. The warehouse burned down on
September 30, a week before. That fire had been at Six-
teenth and State, only a few blocks from her home. "I could
see smoke from my windows," she said honestly.

"Just the warehouse burned up. The fire never crossed
the street."

"Last night," Hallalujah added quickly not to be outdone,

"last night the planing mill burned four square blocks." She didn't tell that she hadn't been allowed to watch it.

"Never crossed a broad street," Rachael said, nodding and hugging Betsy. She smeared the tears across her cheeks.

Hallelujah heard dull fire-wagon bells amid the roar of wind and fire. "The fire fighters, oh, good, they're here!"

The girls dodged around grown-ups running toward the firemen. One woman in her nightgown carried a feather mattress on her head. A barefoot man carried a wooden box of tools. Although the box had a sturdy wooden handle, he hugged it to his chest as if he were holding a baby.

A little girl clutched a noisy clucking chicken and feathers flew as the chicken struggled to go free. Her brother pulled a brown dog on a rope. The dog leaped and barked at the crowd.

Four young women carried cane-bottom chairs, one in each arm. Hallelujah imagined the eight chairs fitting around their kitchen table, but where was the kitchen? Burned up?

Few people were weeping. Most were talking excitedly. Men and women seemed to be comparing how fast their homes had burned down. It seemed most of the poor people along the street had lost their homes to fire.

The girls ran between a mother carrying a colorful thick quilt and her little boy carrying a black iron kettle of water. The little boy could hardly manage the full kettle.

Hallelujah jerked it away from him. She dumped the water on the ground. "Now it's not so heavy," she said, handing it back.

"Mind your own business," the mother yelled. "That was our drinking water."

"Go to your well and drink," Hallelujah yelled back. She

glanced behind to make sure Edward Joseph wasn't around
to tell about her bad manners. "And don't make your little
boy carry such a heavy kettle. Don't you know children get
tired? He's just a little boy born into this world through no
fault of his own."

Rachael opened her mouth in surprise. Grabbing Hallelujah's elbow, Rachael began running and pulling her
away from the woman and child. She seemed ashamed of
Hallelujah. They darted in and out of the crowd until they
reached Harrison Street.

There, horses that pulled three fire wagons were tied to
a tree. The calm horses wore blinders. The ladder truck
stood unused. In back of it a fireman sat wiping his face.

Two other firemen held a hose from the steam boiler
wagon. The flow of water from the pumper was no more
effective than one raindrop in a blazing fireplace. The firemen seemed exhausted. Bleary-eyed with shoulders sagging,
they stood as still as wooden Indians in a cigar store.

"Why aren't they working harder?" Hallelujah called
above the fire wind. "They're just standing there. And that
one's sitting down!"

A woman in a shawl and bonnet rested an arm on her
shoulder. "I reckon they're tired, child."

Rachael pointed at two boys who ran around with kegs
of whiskey. They were offering a drink to everyone they
saw, including the fire fighters. The seated fireman drank
deeply, stared behind him and jumped up.

Hallelujah said, "See, he shouldn't be drinking when
he's on his job. I bet he thinks someone saw him."

"No," Rachael said, "he sees fire. Look!"

At a hoarse yell from this fire fighter, his fellow workers

dropped their hose and rapidly hitched the horses to the fire wagons. The ladder wagon raced away first. The steamer wagon was next. The hose cart was last, dragging its hose as it raced away.

A minute later the dry grass where they had stood was all ablaze. It was as if an artist with flaming yellow color painted in sweeping strokes and sloppy drippings. Fire covered everything behind them. It was wild and thrilling, like nothing Hallelujah had ever seen before.

The crowd surged past Rachael and her. She saw an ocean of fire being blown forward like roaring waves on the lakeshore.

She watched people stream past them. Mothers hugging infants, little girls hugging dolls. A child their size without her bonnet passed carrying an empty bird cage.

"I wonder where her bird is?" Rachael asked.

Hallelujah started after the girl to ask, but Rachael pulled her back. "Never mind, Hallelujah."

Hallelujah stared at the people, wondering. Here, no one knew she was an orphan. Rachael didn't seem to care that she was colored; they were simply children together. That was nice.

The streets were filled with horses pulling drays piled high with cane-bottom chairs, mattresses, pots and pans. A sick man, thin as a skeleton lay on a mattress. He was staring over the side of the flatbed wagon.

People shoved each other aside to keep from being run down by the snorting horses. Hallelujah felt the thuds of running hoofs beneath her shoes.

People here were better dressed. Women wore puffy petticoats under full skirts, fancy bonnets, and lacy shawls around their shoulders. Men wore derbys and even top hats. Rachael pulled back at Hallelujah.

"Look at that furniture!" she said softly. They had reached VanBuren Street and a section of two-story brick homes.

A corner lot was filled with fine stuffed furniture piled high, pictures in frames, and even pianos. One fat lady in purple stood by her piano and held a purple parasol over her head. She was almost as wide as the piano. A large carpetbag lay beside her like a pet dog.

"Think she's expecting rain?" Hallelujah asked, giggling.

"Where's Betsy?" Rachael asked, and glancing down, hugged her doll lovingly on her shoulder.

"Look," said Hallelujah, "there're five pianos and dozens of leather trunks over there."

The fire was two blocks behind them now, and the roar less deafening. She felt excited, but Rachael had slowed down.

"Come on," Hallelujah said, "don't stop now."

But Rachael stared around her. No one else wore torn unbleached cotton. "My mama's looking for me," she said, staring at the clothes on the people around her. Suddenly she glanced down and noticed Hallelujah's brown leather shoes. Rachael was barefoot.

"Mr. Joseph is a shoemaker, that's all," Hallelujah said to explain her handsome shoes. "Come on."

Rachael seemed more overwhelmed by the wealthy people than she had been by the windblown fire. "Me and Betsy going home," she called, "I don't belong here. These are rich folks."

"Hey, these people just got clothes and shoes different," explained Hallelujah. "All of us are people born into this world through no fault of our own. Ain't we?"

Rachael drew back hugging her doll across her chest. Before Hallelujah could grab her, Rachael had run away. Hallelujah took several steps after her, and stopped. Rachael weaved in and out of the crowd as she raced away.

"Good-bye, Rachael," she called, and a chill of loneliness settled over her like dew after midnight. Were these rich people here really different? Shanty homes and sheds had disappeared in flames like sugar melting in hot water, but now the fire was in a better section of town. Should she go home? No one had noticed her back there among the shanties. Was she less of a person than Rachael who was white? Did woolly hair and dark skin make her inferior? Did being an orphan without a living mother or father make her inferior? Was she trash as Edward Joseph had said?

Now she felt miserable. The crowds were headed for the South Branch of the Chicago River, which she had crossed earlier to reach the fire. Oh, well, she thought, I'll go home this way.

People marched along dragging their possessions in trunks. Hallelujah tried imagining what was in the brown leather trunks.

Pretty pink silk dresses to swish down the streets? Fine chinaware to tinkle as people sipped hot tea? Shiny silverware to clink on china plates and lift sweet cakes to the mouth? This game of imagining made her feel less lonely.

Boys were throwing stones to break windows in houses where people seemed to be sleeping. She picked up a stone, but she was afraid to throw it. Suppose someone saw her? Mr. Joseph would be furious, and Miss Tilly would be so ashamed.

When angry people appeared at broken windows, the boys yelled, "Fire!"

She laughed. Who wouldn't know there was a fire? But when she passed a Methodist Church, people inside were singing at late Sunday services. They didn't seem to know. Maybe she should tell them? She might be doing them a favor.

Running up the steps, she dragged open the heavy wooden doors, and shoved a stick under one door to keep it open.

"Fire," she called. "Big wind blowing! Big fire burning!"

People turned in their seats to stare at her. She ran away. This really was fun. She sure hoped none of Mr. Joseph's clients were in there, or any ladies who knew Miss Tilly.

Maybe she should throw her stone, too. Edward Joseph and she often skipped stones at Lake Michigan. She loved throwing pebbles. Her fire was about over now, she thought. These rich people's brick homes wouldn't dare burn down like shanties had. She should throw it while she could, while the fire was still burning. Why not?

She ran ahead and threw her stone. The man who stared out his broken window looked past her. "Mister," she called, "your roof is on fire!" It was, too. Just a little flame.

The man slammed his window shut. In seconds he was on a porch staring up. He wore a long nightshirt, a nightcap, and leather slippers. He ran back inside calling his family to wake up. She picked up more stones. This was fun!

She woke up another family, and another. At the next house the mother called her thanks. Hallelujah felt good about breaking windows and being thanked for it. How often could a child do that? What a great night! What adventure!

She was proud that she had good aim. Her practice at the lake was paying off.

She glanced behind her. At a distance the fat lady in purple hustled clumsily off the empty lot leaving her piano. The entire lot was a sea of fire, burning pianos, trunks, fine carved-wood furniture, pictures in frames. All at once the fire washed over them.

The southwest wind in Hallelujah's face blew pieces of flaming cloth and chunks of blazing hay high above her head. It was new for burning objects to fly through the air.

A moment before, two blocks behind her had been dark and dreary. Now the blocks were bright and shiny yellow from fire.

"The river," said a well-dressed gentleman in top hat and pin-striped pants. He passed her. "The only thing that will stop this fire is the river."

"Well, that's not far," she called to him. "But they said a broad street would stop it, too. And they were wrong."

Frowning at her for answering him, he told her firmly, "The river will stop it, nigger child." He cleared his throat and hurried ahead to catch up with his friend.

She passed the firemen. They had pulled the hitched horses and wagons onto a side street. They were sitting and watching the sky. She crossed the street to give them a scolding.

Edward Joseph's warning tinkled in her ears. She wasn't to cause "nobody no trouble." She twitched her tan skirt nervously. Was asking them why they weren't doing their job causing trouble?

As she approached the ladder wagon, the firemen leaped off. They lashed the waiting horses and raced away again. Turning, she stared behind her into the wind. That wind was lifting heat and flames skyward like a child on a long rope swing.

The fire no longer burned one street, one block at a time. It was playing leapfrog. It rode piggyback on the wind. The entire section behind and beside her was burning all at once.

This wasn't right. Fires weren't supposed to do that. Confused but still thrilled, she ran for the river.

Chapter Five

AS HALLELUJAH RAN, DODGING LOADS ON wagons and squeezing between people, she heard a big shout. The shout was followed by a moan that seemed to come from hundreds of throats at once. As she drew closer, she heard the words: "Across the river!"

She turned and told people hurrying behind her, "Across the river!" Like a town gossip, she told everyone she saw, and they passed it on.

"What's across the river?" asked a tall man. He was holding a beaver fur hat on his head as if it were his good luck charm.

Suddenly Hallelujah herself wondered what it meant. She tugged on a young lady's expensive green taffeta dress. "Pardon, ma'am, but what's across the river?"

The lady reached for her hand. She might have been Mary Jane's age, and she wore soft white gloves. With her other hand she pointed for Hallelujah.

"The fire!"

"I thought so," Hallelujah said. "A man told me the fire would stop at the river, but he was wrong."

"Fire across the river?" The man let go his top hat and it promptly blew off his head. He chased away after it. Hallelujah watched it roll on the wooden sidewalk, lift in the air, and fly amidst dusty trash and dry leaves.

"With wind like this, it's no wonder," she said.

The lady's gloves were so warm and soft that Hallelujah felt safe and happy holding her hand. They were still together when they reached the Adam Street viaduct and bridge over the Chicago river.

"What's your name?" the lady asked.

Hallelujah took a deep breath. "My name is Hallelujah. I was born into this world at sunrise on Easter Sunday through no fault of my own. My father named me Hallelujah, and my mother and father are both dead!"

"What a beautiful name, Hallelujah!"

She relaxed. The lady accepted her name.

"Your parents must love you very much."

"They're dead, I said. Dead!"

"From heaven. They must love you. You're special with a name like Hallelujah. My mother died the day after I was born. In the face of death she named me Hope."

Hallelujah felt wonderful. This pretty rich lady understood after all. An orphan child with brown skin and woolly black hair could still be special! She wasn't trash as Edward Joseph said.

She had come only to watch the fire, but she was meeting interesting people who were as fascinating as the fire. There was so much to think about with Rachael and with this lady named Hope.

Before them fire danced crazily on both sides of the river. Hand in hand she and Hope strolled casually onto the broad

iron bridge. The man who lost his top hat joined them.
He said, "Nothing can stop it now!"

Hallelujah turned and passed his words along. "They say
nothing can stop it now!" she called. As she said it, she
skipped happily. What a wonderful adventure, she thought.
The lady named Hope frowned at her gently and shook her
head.

At the Canal Street embankment she saw where the
planing mill fire the night before had scorched the ground
black. There was nothing more to burn. It was as bare as
a swept floor.

All around her people moaned. They kept repeating,
"Nothing can stop it now!"

She peeked over the bridge railing. Boats of all sizes were
passing on the river. Sailors scrambled throwing bits of
burning trash into the water. The water hissed as it put out
the burning straw and cloth and paper.

The man said, "Firebrands and cinders. They'll carry the
fire."

Hallelujah watched the wind swirl firebrands, burning
wood, in the air like a clown juggler. She watched huge
chunks of heavy burning hay fly lightly overhead. Below
her on the river, brigs, sloops, barges, propellers, barques,
schooners, and bigger steam engine boats floated by in a
busy stream.

One captain's clothes caught on fire. He promptly leaped
into the water. Hallelujah laughed, and after a shocked
moment, Hope smiled as the wet captain climbed back onto
his boat.

"Aren't you worried?" asked Hope.

"No, ma'am," said Hallelujah. "I laughed because my

foster brother works at the grain port loading wheat and corn. That was Captain Hunter Jones. I'll have to tell Edward Joseph that story."

Her conscience stabbed her. She remembered yelling at Edward Joseph before she ran away. She didn't mean what she said, and she knew he didn't mean what he said either.

"I mean worried about the fire?"

Before she could answer, the gentleman said, "Can you believe that?"

"What?" asked Hallelujah.

He pointed. "Brick buildings fire-torched like paper. I thought sure stone and brick would stand up to this fire. Some of that limestone is from Lemont. It's melting down like sugar!"

Sure enough expensive row houses of cream-colored stone seemed to crumble in the flames. Burning felt from flat roofs lifted piece by piece and flew ahead to set fire to other buildings.

"It's the wind," Hallelujah said. "Mr. Post said this was no night for a fire!"

She felt happy that these people were treating her with respect, listening to her. They seemed to forget she was a child, and colored.

A gentleman behind them in the crowd said, "*Tribune* wrote about shabby Chicago construction. Just last month the *Tribune* said it. Some of these buildings are only one brick thick."

Hope told them: "A cornice fell off a bank building and just missed me. All that stone just toppled off and crashed to the street. Lucky no one was under it." She shook her head. "This town just grew too fast, they say."

"It grew too fast, and the ground is too dry, and the wind is too strong," Hallelujah added. She skipped a step. How excited she felt. After throwing the stones, she had been tired, but now she felt lively again.

Explosions began. "Beeswax!" she shouted.

She pulled free and stopped to hold both hands over her ears. She didn't mean to leave Hope, but she was jostled away from the white gloves. Hope. Now that was a great name, and it meant so much.

Bang! Crash! Bang! Boom! Crash!

"The gasworks are blowing up," a deep voice called. She passed the word along. "The gasworks are blowing up!" But she wondered why so many bangs?

The earth trembled under her shoes. The very sky seemed ablaze with flying fire. People around her grew hushed. No chatter. No calls. Just feet marching on dusty streets, horses whinnying as they pulled carts and wagons. Infants even stopped crying. She didn't know what to think. Awe and wonder overcame her.

Soon she found herself at the handsome five-story courthouse building where the bell tower rang out all sorts of Chicago news. Set on a large city block, the courthouse was bounded by LaSalle, Clark, Randolph, and Washington streets.

It was tall and noble, surrounded by trees and gardens. Built of creamy Lemont, Illinois, limestone, it had courts and offices on the top floors and the city jail in the basement.

The fire bell and news bells rang from there.

Hallelujah remembered Miss Tilly telling how the bells rang when President Abraham Lincoln was killed. Edward

Joseph and Mary Jane had gone with Miss Tilly to see President Lincoln in his coffin. He had lain in state at this fine courthouse. That had been six years before, and she had been too young to go.

LaSalle Street had special meaning for her too because she lived with the LaSalles. Now the buildings on both sides of LaSalle Street were blazing orange and yellow.

Before President Abraham Lincoln freed the slaves with the Emancipation Proclamation, Mr. Joseph's name had been Smith. A Smith family in Tennessee had owned his parents before they escaped to Chicago.

After freedom for all colored people, Mr. Joseph promised himself a new name: a free name, not a slave name. He walked Chicago streets looking for a new name. He liked the creamy limestone banks and handsome Greek architecture of the commercial buildings along LaSalle Street. He and Miss Tilly decided to take LaSalle for their last name.

That memory forced tears to spring into Hallelujah's eyes. She really loved Mr. Joseph and Miss Tilly. She hadn't realized how much! And now their beautiful Chicago Courthouse was burning.

Suddenly this fire wasn't fun anymore. Buildings were being burned down, important buildings. She began to feel guilty for wanting a big fire. Had God answered her prayer with this fire? Was she responsible? If so, she had to stop God.

She raised her face and called into the noisy wind: "Lord, listen to me and stop this fire. This is me, Hallelujah, born on Easter Sunday. I'm sorry for wanting to see a big fire. Please, stop!" She listened and stared around, but nothing changed.

The mean old fire was destroying things, and that wasn't right. How could she have felt happy when she watched people's homes burn down? She felt ashamed of herself now, but she had been so excited then!

She stood among a crowd of hushed, well-dressed, rich people. Men held high hats and gold-headed canes. Their gray or black suits were pressed. Ladies had bonnets with ribbons of satin. Some of their autumn dresses were sewn of velvet and their silk shawls had lace on the edges.

She stared around her. These were rich folks, millionaires maybe; what were they really like? Boldly, she edged over to a slender girl a little taller than she was.

The girl carried a fancy dressed doll with painted shoes on its china feet, and a painted smile on its china face. The girl and her doll were dressed alike. Her blue bonnet had lace; the doll's blue bonnet had lace. Both wore blue taffeta dresses.

"What's your doll's name?" Halleujah asked.

"Betsy," the girl whispered. She stared into Hallelujah's bonnet by firelight and saw her brown face. "Do you have a doll?"

"Yes. Her name is Suzy. I met another girl tonight with a doll named Betsy."

"Really? Well, her name is Elizabeth in full. My papa's gone to fetch our carriage. Then we'll go visit relatives in Oak Park. My mother's nervous."

"I live in the South Division," Hallelujah said to keep the conversation going. She had never talked to a rich child before.

"My house is in the North Division. We're quite safe. I'm so lucky my mama let me come to the fire."

"Me, too," said Hallelujah. "The other Betsy doll was a corncob doll."

"Corncob? How odd. What's your doll like?"

"She's carved from wood. Mr. Joseph made it for my birthday."

"A wooden doll? Does it bend?"

"No, but her arms are on pegs. I can move her arms back and forth. Can I hold your doll?"

The girl in blue taffeta backed away. "No. Not really. You see, she cost a lot of money. My papa brought her from France."

She accidentally backed into her mother. The well-dressed mother took one glance at Hallelujah and snatched her child away. She scolded, "Don't you know what she is? She's a nigger. You shouldn't talk to niggers!"

Hallelujah stood firm and watched. She felt angry. They weren't any better than she was. Were they?

As the mother dragged her away, the girl smiled and wiggled her fingers good-bye. That made Hallelujah feel better. She smiled and waved wildly. She had made another friend. What an interesting night!

She stood staring after the rich child, and the crowd parted, leaving her standing alone.

A man moved forward and tapped her shoulder. "Child, make way for the prisoners. They're freeing the prisoners from jail."

Her first thought was, I'm glad someone thought about them. They're people, too!

She wondered what prisoners looked like? At the edge of the crowd, she stood and watched for them.

Chapter Six

AS IF DEVILISH IMPS WERE INSIDE, TONGUES OF scarlet flame licked out every window of the handsome Chicago Courthouse. The building was bright, and in a terrifying way, more beautiful than Hallelujah had ever seen it in sunlight.

The jail was in the basement. She stared at the doors, and wished the prisoners would hurry out. She glanced down LaSalle Street. Stone and brick buildings five and seven stories high were toppling in the fire the same as wooden buildings had in the West Division. Streets were as bright as high noon in July. The crowd was hushed.

Here, families stood by piles of books, and boxes, and desk drawers from offices. Architects, surveyors, bankers, and newsmen from the *Chicago Tribune* and the *Chicago Evening Post* gathered in unhappy groups watching their buildings crumble to rubble in the fire. Thumps and thuds shook the ground.

A woman in a black dress and bonnet raised a Bible high. "Repent and be saved! It's the end of the world," she called. She waved the Bible.

No one seemed to pay her much attention.

From where she stood Hallelujah saw the building where Mr. Joseph worked. His cobbler shop had been in the basement of a large commercial building on Washington Street. But the building was gone now, burned to the ground.

A gentleman held a gold pocket watch in one hand. In his other hand he carried his things in a carpetbag. He told his friend who wore a brown derby, "The gasworks blew up at one-thirty. The Armory's gone. Wells Street is on fire as far as Monroe."

His friend said: "And they're opening the bridges for tall schooners. People are trapped in the West Division. The wind is strong. I don't know where it'll end."

As they were speaking, a boy named Jay Sky from Hallelujah's school bumped her elbow. He was tall and slender with a flat brown face and slanted Indian eyes.

"Edward Joseph is searching for you, Hallelujah. Looking all over the West Division."

"So what?" She glanced nervously around him to see if Edward Joseph were there. Was he trapped in the West Division as the man had said?

Jay Sky said, "My people say fires like this happen. Make the land rich for new crops, better than before."

"Well, some people are saying it's the end of the world."

He shook his head. "The world stretches far. This is only Chicago burning." Brushing past her shoulder lightly, he moved on, slipping through the crowd like a cat's shadow.

Hallelujah felt better. She was honored that he had spoken to her. At school when he was teased, she always took up for him, even though he was a boy. He had never thanked her.

Mr. Joseph had told her that Jean Baptiste du Sable, the colored fur trader who was the first settler to live at Chicago, married an Indian lady. Indians were the first people in America, but they were treated shamefully. At least, she thought, they were never slaves.

Turning, Hallelujah stared at the pocket watch the gentleman held right under her eyes. It read 2:15. She had never been out that late at night before.

"Here they come." A whisper stirred among the people.

The grounds of the courthouse showed people running. The prisoners were mostly men: some in overalls, some in cheap suits, some in fine pinstripes. The few ladies, dressed in bright colors, ran out crying. All the prisoners seemed eager to put space between them and the burning building.

Hallelujah saw no children and was disappointed. It would have been interesting to talk to a child from jail.

As she stared, the courthouse began to crumble. She wondered how this wonderful stone building where Abraham Lincoln had lain in state could burn down? Was this really the end of the world? For a second time tears spurted in her eyes like waters from a spring.

The grand cupola where the bell hung began to sway like willow branches in the wind. She thought maybe her eyes were seeing things. Then with an enormous thud the cupola toppled to the ground and many stones followed. Slowly the walls collapsed.

"Twenty minutes," said the man with the gold watch. He snapped it closed. "The grand Chicago Courthouse burned down in just twenty minutes!"

With a hissing sigh the crowds moved on, but she stood crying. She wiped her eyes on her sleeve. This fire was destructive; it wasn't fair. All of downtown Chicago was on fire, and still the wind blew.

Sadly she raised her face: "Listen to me, Lord. You helped my mama walk all the way up here to Chicago. Help Chicago now!" Closing her eyes, she yelled, "Stop the fire, God!" Listening, she half expected the roar of fire to quiet, but it didn't She opened her eyes. Apparently God wasn't as easy to handle as Mr. Joseph was.

She turned and started home. She had seen enough. Walking slowly to State Street, she headed south. She passed a pile of books in the street. The books were *Oliver Twist, David Copperfield, Swiss Family Robinson.* She stared at the titles, but she was too tired and felt too sad to stoop and pick them up.

On State Street downtown, tall stores were still standing. Wagons carrying kegs and crates from department stores were burning even as the drivers tried to escape the crowded streets. Poor people ran and stole clothes and furniture out of open stores. Then they skipped away leaving the chairs and clothes in flames in the street.

The crowds here were frantic. Ladies' full skirts caught flames and men beat the fires out. Children screamed in fear.

The fine hotels were on fire. Grand hotels like the Briggs House, the Sherman, the newly built Palmer House, and the Tremont. Crosby's Opera House was on fire. Hallelujah saw Field and Leiter's sparkling new marble-front department store on State Street all aflame. Men were dragging yards of cloth, overcoats, hats, and gloves outside the burning building. And outside the clothes caught fire from firebrands. There was no escaping this fire.

Two fire trucks clanged on their way to the lake. People laughed at them. Hallelujah felt angry that they should laugh at the poor fire fighters, although she remembered wanting to scold them herself.

"Don't you understand?" she screamed. "They were tired. You would have been tired, too, if you had fought fires all week!"

A shop girl roughly beat at her shoulder. Hallelujah turned to knock her arm off. Was she attacking her?

"Fire!" called the young woman.

Hallelujah's dress had been on fire. Now she could smell the burnt cotton, feel the heat. "Thank you," she called.

"Watch your skirts," the young woman said. She twitched her skirt and showed several burned places.

Hallelujah began to tremble. Now the fire was a threat. She herself had been on fire! She said, "Thank you," again.

"Never no bother," the immigrant girl said. "You was right." She pointed after the fire trucks. "The only way they could've stopped this here fire, was iffen they had caught it before it began."

Hallelujah nodded. Why hadn't she said that?

A man in cap and work trousers waved. "Have you heard?"

"Heard what, sir?" she answered. He had actually spoken to her. During a fire people seemed more human; some of them, anyway.

Self-conscious, self-centered, Hallelujah had seen the fire at first as entertainment. Now the horror broke through in small spurts; she was a foolish little girl, but growing wiser.

The man said, "The waterworks are destroyed. There was a wooden roof over them four great big pumps, and it burned down. No water in the pipes. Firemen have to use the lake waters."

The immigrant girl ran over. "Oh, God," she called. "There's no hope now!"

Hallelujah had known a lady named Hope that night. "There's always hope," she said. "A fire can only burn until it can't burn anymore."

She grew dizzy and kept blinking. Every time she closed her eyes it was harder and harder to open them again. Her eyes seemed filled with grit.

"You're right," called the immigrant girl.

Hallelujah felt dazed and confused. Her eyes could hardly see through the smoke billowing around her now, so she closed her eyes. Home seemed so far away. Could she ever reach it?

For a while she walked without looking, and she stumbled on something. When she opened her eyes, she saw at her feet a fine feather mattress and a pile of blue blankets. They must have dropped off a wagon.

She pushed and pulled the mattress away from the crowd toward an alleyway between buildings, and then she crawled on it.

Since no one could stop the fire, why should Hallelujah worry? She fell soundly asleep.

Chapter Seven

HALLELUJAH AWAKENED TO A SERIES OF EXPLO-sions like guns shooting. The stench of burning feathers filled her nostrils, and made her cough. She felt burning heat and saw that her mattress was like a decorated quilt of orange and blue smoldering flames. Fire was creeping up on her. She felt a stabbing pain on her back. She jumped off the mattress.

For several minutes she beat at flames on her skirt, flames on her bonnet. She was terrified. Screaming, she backed away twisting and turning. Her back pained sharply. She was on fire!

A gentleman snuffed out the burning hole on her back. He said, "Go home, child. You're not burning anywhere else."

"Thank you," she said. She checked her sleeves, her skirt. She put on her bonnet again to keep her hair from catching on fire. The man had kept her from burning.

He didn't care about her age or her color. Even in pain, she was self-conscious. She trembled. Before she left, she picked up one of the blankets in the pile near the mattress. Maybe it could help her if she caught on fire again. Her back pained sharply.

The explosions continued, sharp shooting sounds. Everything noisy had sounded dull while she slept. Now it was loud again. She must hurry home.

She had only walked half a block when someone called her by name. It was her mother's friend, Mr. Thomas Baker. The same Mr. Baker from whom she had hidden Sunday afternoon. What was he doing here?

"Where's your papa, Hallelujah?"

"Mr. Joseph is home I think, sir."

"Then you take this. It be important. You a small child for a big sack, but you a strong-hearted child. I know that." He handed her a heavy canvas sack tied with stout cord.

He told her, "Don't let no flames get it, you hear?"

"No, sir. Where shall I take it?" she asked as they were pushed around by the crowd.

By now burning cinders fell as thick as hail. Smoke no longer cleared in the sky. Billows of black smoke swept along the streets. Chunks of flaming doors and blazing hay barely missed Hallelujah's bonnet. The heat was unbearable. Every few minutes she beat at burning spots on her shoulders and skirt. She had to make sure she wasn't on fire. Should she tell Mr. Baker that her back had a burn?

A screaming woman ran past them all aflame. Another woman grabbed a blanket off a pile in the street, and wrestled her to the ground. She put out the fire, but the woman moaned from the painful burns.

Hallelujah trembled and wrapped the heavy sack in her blanket. They stepped aside from the crowd. She was confused with so much going on all around them.

"Where shall I take it?" she asked again.

He pointed east. "You takes it right out there to the lake and you waits for me. You hear?"

How did she know if he would come back? By then her eyelids and throat burned from smoke, and all she wanted to do was lie down and sleep. She could hardly keep her eyes open.

"What time is it?" she asked. They stood next to each other but she had to shout. Explosions banged continually.

"Now, never you mind," Mr. Thomas Baker told her. "Them bangs is barrels of oil blowing up. But this here bag be real important. Now I got two hands free to go back for two more. Just you stand out by that lake and try not to wet this bag. But don't let it catch on fire, neither."

She answered, "Yes, sir." And he hurried off.

At no other time, for no other person would she have been so agreeable. But Mr. Baker was like a guardian, always checking up on her and Mary Jane, and how they were doing in Chicago. And he *had* called her a strong-hearted child.

As she turned east on VanBuren Street, her legs seemed as loose as floppy earthworms. She hoped she could make it to the lake. How she wanted to go home to Miss Tilly and her own bed. How she wanted to sleep! How her back pained!

She passed Wabash Street. People on Wabash seemed to have gone crazy. Bottles of whiskey littered the sidewalk. Drunken men and women were dancing in the street. Children ran about laughing and beating at burning cinders for a game. Other people were setting things on fire.

She stared. Yes! Men, women, and children were carrying flaming torches and setting furniture on fire. Setting

piles of books from shopkeepers and accountants on fire!
They were adding more fire to the disaster.

She screamed at them: "Stop that. Can't you see what's
happening? Why are you making more trouble?"

Luckily, they couldn't hear her above the roar.

A boy saw her waving, and ran toward her. Drunken and
laughing, he poked a board to set her on fire. She ran away
from him. As she ran, she shifted the sack to the top of
her shoulder. Mr. Thomas Baker said it was important, but
the sack made her clumsy.

She wanted to ask why she was protecting the sack for
Mr. Baker, but she knew.

Mr. Thomas Baker was from Provident Baptist Church,
her church. He was a kind man, and he had asked her to
do a favor for him. He had done a great favor for her mother.
Now Hallelujah could repay him.

Provident Baptist was where her mother found refuge
after running away to the north. Mr. Baker arranged for
Sophia, her mother, and Hallelujah, who was only an infant, and Mary Jane, who was five years old, to live with
Miss Tilly and Mr. Joseph. His job as a deacon was to help
slaves who made it to Chicago.

Of course, that was just before the War Between the
States; before the LaSalles bought the house at Twelfth and
State.

After the war, Sophia lived with her girls in the same
room where Hallelujah and Mary Jane slept now. Her
mother had worked at Armour's Meat Packing Company
where Miss Tilly and Mary Jane worked.

But her mother never recovered from the cold walk up
north. Industrial Chicago's heavy smoke—the smoke of

"progress"—had ruined her weakened lungs. She got sick, had coughed blood, and finally had died.

Hallelujah blinked back tears. Mr. Baker had helped her mother, and she would help him. She didn't need to ask why. She didn't even need to know what was in the sack.

At any other time curiosity would have made her peek. It was heavy and squishy, but not soft. She knew how tired she was when she didn't have the strength to untie the sack. She just didn't care. She was doing a favor for Mr. Baker, and that was enough.

She had escaped the boy with fire, but she was still angry. Setting fires in a fire storm! What kind of people made trouble, when other people needed help? Her conscience stabbed her with a sharp memory. She did. That very day she had argued with Miss Tilly when the Sullivans needed her to take them food. She wanted to tattle on her sister and brother. She worried Mr. Joseph.

She bit her lip and walked faster through billowing smoke and showering cinders. Faces everywhere were smudged with black soot. Her tan dress was blackened with soot. The burn on her back pained. From time to time she checked to make sure she wasn't on fire.

She reached Michigan Avenue. Homes along Michigan Avenue across the sandy park from Lake Michigan, were owned by millionaires. Flames licked hungrily at these homes, too.

Fine limestone houses, three stories high, on fire. The street full of loaded wagons, on fire. Furniture piled high, on fire. Trunks of clothing, on fire.

Tears on wealthy people's faces made light streaks down sooty blackened cheeks.

She passed rich people attending to poor immigrants, and poor people helping the rich. One rich lady held a child in tattered clothing in each arm and had skinny, raggedly dressed children clinging to her skirt. The lady seemed to wear pain carved into her face.

The children wept and pointed to their mother lying still under fallen stones. Fires licked at the dead mother's dress.

Hallelujah winced and hugged one of the little girls.

"Where's your papa?" Hallelujah asked.

"Long dead," said the little girl.

Hallelujah said quickly, "It's all right to be an orphan. Don't let people make you feel like a nobody. I'm an orphan too. We're children same as others." She hugged the little girl again.

As she hurried away she thought, What a silly thing to say. I talk too much. But it's true. She walked half a block. More and more she was beginning to realize how foolish differences were. People were all the same.

Those children's mother was the first dead person she had noticed. Now in front of her were seven other blackened bodies lying near burned rubble. They might have been colored; they might have been white. No one could tell. She started to scream but she covered her mouth with the sack.

Dead people. Colored or white, rich or poor, recent immigrant or longtime citizen; in death they all looked alike. Dead people. And how awful the burned flesh smelled!

One was a child her size who might have been a classmate. She hugged the heavy sack tighter. Children were actually dying in this fire. Dead bodies terrified her. She began to tremble and feel frantic, but she remembered, "Go to the lake. Stand by the water."

In her mind she heard Mr. Baker's voice, and she obeyed. At the sight of dead bodies, she wanted to scream and cry and run. But she held herself together. She obeyed.

Chapter Eight

LAKE WATERS LEAPED IN THE WIND. THE LAKE was only about 300 feet east of Michigan Avenue. Several families had driven horses and carriages out into the water. Children huddled next to their mothers and fathers and peered from carriage windows.

Loaded wagons pulled by horses formed wooden islands in the lake. Merchants on the wagons kept wetting down their crates to keep them from catching fire. Dogs stood guard by barrels.

In sad clusters, fathers, mothers, and children stood knee-deep in the lake facing the burning city. Rich families. Colored families. Poor families. Working people families. Business people families. Immigrant families. Danger threatened all equally.

How cool the lake water would feel on her burned back. She raised her shoulders to relieve the pain a little.

As Hallelujah stood on the lakeshore, her loneliness won over the burning pain, and she said hello to a chubby girl who carried a bird cage. This child was ash dirty over a yellow satin dress and bonnet. She must have been out to something fancy like an opera that night. Over her shoulders she wore a yellow-and-green plaid wool shawl.

The girl stared at Hallelujah's brown face, and did not answer. Inside the cage she clutched tightly, a nervous yellow canary hopped from perch to perch.

Undaunted, Hallelujah asked, "What's your bird's name?"

"I don't talk to niggers," the girl said.

"Why don't you try covering him with your shawl? Then maybe the smoke won't get him."

The girl stared at Hallelujah. Slowly and cautiously she handed her the cage. She removed her plaid shawl and wrapped it gently around her pet's cage. After she took the cage back, she peeked under the shawl every few seconds.

"Where's your folks?" Hallelujah asked.

The girl didn't answer. She could take Hallelujah's suggestion, but she couldn't speak to her. Hallelujah felt lonelier than ever, but not discouraged. The fire was teaching her her worth.

Smoke billowed around them and everything was black. Hallelujah heard the canary drop from its perch with a plop. The girl began to scream and wail. Her shrill screaming made Hallelujah's burn pain more. She couldn't stand it. Hallelujah felt like screaming herself. She moved away from the girl.

Wind blew Hallelujah aside. People leaped and beat at cinders that landed on their clothes.

From one space to another, Hallelujah slinked like a wary fox in the hunter's woods. More and more people were backing into the water. She didn't want to wet her school shoes. Adjusting the blanket, she hugged the heavy sack tighter.

When a brown horse and carriage with fringed top drove in, she moved farther down the lakeshore. Her body felt as if heavy stones weighed her down.

"Hello!"

Hallelujah turned and stared. Through soot on the girl's face she recognized the rich child from the courthouse fire. "Hello. What are you doing here? Where's your mama?"

"We were going to Oak Park when our carriage caught fire. My papa took us off to put out the flames, and the horse ran away. The last I saw, he was running after it. Then I got lost in the crowd and couldn't find my mother."

"Why did you come here?"

The girl pointed. "My grandparents lived there. I thought I could stay with them, but they already left. Nobody is here, not even a servant." A sob shook her.

Hallelujah put an arm around her. "That's all right. You can come home with me."

"Do you think so?"

Hallelujah stared at the girl. Her fancy blue taffeta dress was sooty black. Her long yellow hair was sooty black. Her face was sooty black. Only her pale blue eyes were clear.

Hallelujah told her, "Besides, no one could tell who you are now. What's your name, anyway?"

"Elizabeth Farwell. What's yours?" Black smoke billowed around them.

Hallelujah took a deep breath. "Hallelujah. Born at sunrise on Easter Sunday. You Christian?"

Elizabeth nodded, taken aback by her loud impatient voice.

"Well, then you understand. Hallelujah! Jews understand, too. Angels sing Hallelujah." How she hated defending her name.

She grew angry defending her name, but she was intensely

loyal to it. All she had in legacy from her dead parents was her life, her name, and her presence in Chicago.

Elizabeth said, "It's a nice name."

Hallelujah relaxed. "Where's your pretty china doll?"

"I lost Betsy, too." At this Elizabeth began to cry.

"That's all right. I'm sure your papa will buy you another French doll."

"No," she called between sobs. "I'm crying because I'm so sorry I didn't let you hold her. Now I don't even have Betsy anymore! I dropped her somewhere, and couldn't find her."

Serves you right, Hallelujah thought. Then she was sorry for thinking it. She shifted the sack and put an arm around Elizabeth.

Her movement rubbed the burned spot on her back and she winced. She couldn't help thinking that she was bearing the pain well. She *was* a strong-hearted girl!

"You were right," she said. "Your doll cost a lot of money and for all you knew I might have taken your Betsy and run away."

"No, I really didn't think that. It was just that . . . Well, you're . . . anyway, I've never known . . . anyone brown like you before."

Hallelujah nodded. "And I've never known anyone rich like you before." She brushed ash off Elizabeth's shoulder and checked her own bonnet and skirt.

Ah! she thought. This girl was able to talk about real things. She couldn't wait to ask her some questions.

Elizabeth wiped her nose on a lacy handkerchief from a pocket, and pointed. "I saw a lady have her baby right over there in the sand."

Envy choked Hallelujah. How she wished she could have

seen that. "That's silly of her," she said. "Why would she want to have a baby on a night like this?" She beat at a red cinder on her skirt.

Elizabeth frowned at her. "Well, maybe she didn't have any choice. Don't you know about babies? When they come, they come! Didn't your mother ever have a baby?"

"No. My real mother's dead, and Miss Tilly is too old, I think. Anyway she only had Edward Joseph, and he's grown and working. But the Sullivans next door to us have babies all the time." Hallelujah tried to ease the pain on her back.

She failed to tell that she was never allowed to go next door during births. Sometimes Miss Tilly helped deliver babies. And Mary Jane boiled water and wrung hot cloths. But for Hallelujah it was all hush, hush!

"My mother gives birth in our birthing room."

"Birthing room?"

"Yes. It's a special room where the doctor goes to help her. Don't your Sullivans have a birthing room?"

Hallelujah sighed and said, "No."

The Sullivans were so crowded in their house with sixteen people, there wasn't a special room for anything. Grandparents slept in their dining room; parents slept in their parlor; and some of the children had cots in the kitchen.

Hallelujah realized that she could hardly make a child like Elizabeth understand this. Elizabeth probably lived in a big house with only her small family and their servants.

Elizabeth's grandparents lived on Terrace Row. This row of houses on Michigan Avenue between VanBuren and Congress streets was among the most luxurious of living places. Only the wealthy lived there. The really rich. And now their homes were burning, too.

"Look out!" a man shouted from nearby. "Watch that Teuton."

Hallelujah and Elizabeth turned to look.

A muscular man in burned shirt and trousers had begun to fight a gentleman in striped gray pants. The German was opening his mouth, but above the roar of wind and fire, they couldn't hear what he was yelling.

Several men joined in the struggle. The soot-covered German immigrant ran scattering people's bundles. Men and boys chased him. Hallelujah hugged her bag with both arms. She dug her feet more firmly in the sand.

Elizabeth told her: "Just drop that bag and let's move out of the way of that crazy man. Besides, if I catch fire, you have to beat it out."

"No," Hallelujah said. "Don't try to boss me around."

"What's in there anyway?"

"None of your business." How could she explain that she didn't know?

Finally the German came near and began to beat a horse with his fists. Hallelujah screamed: "Stop that! You're mean! Don't you see how terrible we all feel?"

Elizabeth stepped behind her.

The man heard Hallelujah and turned toward her. Now she recognized him. He was Mr. Schneider who owned a hardware store in the same building with Mr. Joseph's shoe-making shop. The German started for her, his eyes glazed with anger. She backed up the shoreline quickly.

Before he reached her, two men wrestled him to the sand. A group of men and boys carried him into the lake and dunked him. He rose out of the waters weeping. Sobbing, he raised his arms in the air.

"I lost everything," he explained in English.

Now the girls were close enough to hear.

"My wife, my children, burned to death. My house, my store, my wagons, my horses, all burned up. Everything!"

Elizabeth tried to pull Hallelujah away from listening to the sobbing man, but Hallelujah stepped forward slowly.

"I'm sorry, Mr. Schneider," she called. "Lots of folks have lost their loved ones tonight. At least you're not alone."

He stared at her as she backed away. "Poor man," she said.

"He's the first person I've seen who went mad," said Elizabeth. She shook her taffeta skirt and brushed her bonnet.

"You're right," Hallelujah said. "I just had to tell him I was sorry." Her painful back made her realize that she had been hurt by the fire, too. They walked toward a clump of kneeling women. An infant cried.

"A newborn," Elizabeth said happily. "Another lady had a baby!"

"I still think it's a silly time to have a baby."

Elizabeth pointed. "Is that man waving at you?"

"Who?" Hallelujah hoped Mr. Joseph had come for her. Or Edward Joseph, dear Edward Joseph. But the man on horseback was Mr. Thomas Baker. He swooped down to grab the sack from her. In saddle bags hung two other sacks like hers.

"I thanks you greatly, Miss Hallelujah," he said breathless and smiling. "What's in these bags be important for our city."

He swirled the handsome horse and rode away through the crowd.

Hallelujah felt angry. Why hadn't he offered her a ride home? She turned to Elizabeth.

"That's that. Let's go. My home isn't far."

"Do you think it burned down? Our house burned down."
Hallelujah simply stared at her. With all the fire and
fury, she had never imagined *their* home burning. Why
hadn't she worried? Was she that selfish and thoughtless?

Their beautiful white house on State Street? Burned? Trot-
ting fast, she dragged Elizabeth by the hand. They began
twisting and turning making a path through the crowd.
Behind them Mr. Schneider still shouted and sobbed.

Everyone stared at the girls because they were heading
back to where fire still raged, but new strength flowed in
Hallelujah. She had grown stiff standing still. It felt good
to be moving.

She remembered Mr. Baker's words. He had called her
strong-hearted, and he had called her "miss." The title
"miss" was kept for young ladies who were no longer children, or for rich children of noble parents. It was a title of
respect, and he had called her Miss Hallelujah. Pleased,
she tugged at Elizabeth to run faster.

On Michigan Avenue some carriages were going north,
or thought they were. Other carriages were going south, or
thought they were. Crowds and carriages simply milled
about swatting at fires.

Hallelujah could not be stopped. She dragged Elizabeth
around carriages, between carriages, and they even crawled
under carriages on hands and knees with long skirts hugged
tightly. Hallelujah was going south, and nothing was going
to stop her.

Chapter Nine

HALLELUJAH AND ELIZABETH SAW FIREMEN, their pumper engines steaming. The fire hoses were held down in the lake for water. The spray of water wet down people and buildings near the lake.

"Good for them," said Hallelujah. "They haven't given up."

"They didn't save our great city!" Elizabeth said.

"How could they? With this wind nothing could stop the fire. In fact, the only way they could have stopped this fire, was to have stopped it before it began!"

Hallelujah grew worried. The horror of the fire was enormous, but here she was repeating what someone else had said. Was she only a mindless parrot, repeating what other people said? Didn't she hurt? Didn't she understand what had happened?

Elizabeth said, "They should have saved my house. We had a very handsome house, it was filled with the best in furniture. And it burned down!" Elizabeth began to weep as she walked. Tears made clear trails through the mask of soot on her face. Hallelujah glanced at her. What's wrong with me? She thought. I haven't sobbed like that. And I have a burn hurting my back.

Past Harrison Street fewer buildings were on fire. Hallelujah felt relieved as the wind with less fire behind it, grew cooler and cooler. Their house was about three blocks farther south. It was probably safe after all.

She glanced to the east over the lake. Out of gray tumbling waters she saw a dull red sun rise, dripping hope, she thought.

"Sunrise," she said. "Isn't it beautiful?" Was it all right to see beauty after a night like that?

They stood on the cross street staring at the sunrise. A gentleman passed and announced to anyone who was interested, "It's seven o'clock."

It was seven in the morning on the ninth of October, 1871.

As Hallelujah paused, Elizabeth had a chance to catch her breath. She had been dragged at a furious pace. A chilly breeze made her begin to shiver.

"I don't know," Elizabeth said. "That sun looks too much like fire to seem pretty to me."

Hallelujah said, "It's too far away to burn things."

"You don't understand. Fire burned my house down! We don't have our wonderful house anymore. I hate that sun!"

Hallelujah said wistfully, "I was born at sunrise." With a shuddering sigh, she added, "I used to hate myself and my life. I'm an orphan and a Mississippi slave child. I worried because I didn't feel or act like other people. And, when I felt angry, I acted mean." She shook her head and went on, "I have no right to be mean to people." She thought of Miss Tilly. She thought of Mary Jane and her precious fifty cents.

She asked Elizabeth, "Do you know what I'm talking about?"

Elizabeth said, "All this tonight . . . being out in crowds with ordinary people . . . meeting you . . . makes me feel so different. I don't know what to make of it. It's not what my papa would approve of." She tossed her sooty yellow curls and clenched her fists.

Hallelujah glanced at her and nodded. She bet she knew what Elizabeth meant. Poor Elizabeth was walking home with her, a colored person. Her rich parents would never approve of that.

Elizabeth added, "I'm not the kind of girl for these things to happen to. I've never been around common people like this."

Hallelujah decided that she meant, I'm too good for this.

No cinders rained on them now, but the wind blew dust in their faces. They were beyond the fire.

"Do you ever worry over whether you're worth much?" Hallelujah asked.

"Never!" Elizabeth was still shivering.

"Of course you don't," Hallelujah said with a sigh. "You aren't pitied as an orphan. You aren't called 'nigger' and 'trash' by your foster brother."

"Well," Elizabeth said, tossing her dirty curls airily, "why do you let it bother you? You know who you are."

"Do I? Do you?" Hallelujah sighed. "But, I've made up my mind that I'm not going to let anyone pity me. It's all right to be an orphan, and colored. I'm no worse and no better than any other child. How we act often depends on what we think of ourselves."

She thought, I can think for myself. I'm not being a parrot now. I'm just talkative.

Elizabeth said quickly, "How we act, depends on what we think of others." She shook her head and sighed. "Hallelujah, I never talked like this before. At home this is not how we feel about common people. At our house my mama and papa put people in . . . boxes, but I never liked it."

"Boxes?"

"Yes, like strong but dumb people, lazy and dirty people, low-class people, respectable people with class. Boxes like that."

Hallelujah didn't ask what box they put colored people in. She had enough bad names to deal with. She'd even been born a slave! She said, "You know that fire? It didn't spare anyone."

Elizabeth said sadly, "I saw. And it's too bad it takes a fire storm to allow children to meet and know each other."

"Well," Hallelujah said, beginning to walk again, "there's always hope. Maybe families in Chicago will be different after this. If there is a Chicago after this."

"I will be different," Elizabeth said firmly.

"I will be, too. See," Hallelujah said, "there is hope!"

As they walked, they passed fewer people now. The crowds were behind them. Hallelujah saw neighbors hurrying to work. She spied her sister, Mary Jane.

"Where are you going?" Hallelujah called.

"Where have you been? Miss Tilly's been worried all night." Mary Jane carried a lunch basket on her arm. Again she asked, "Where were you? Why, you're covered with ashes! Why aren't you with Edward Joseph?"

She stared at Hallelujah and Hallelujah stared at her.

Again Hallelujah asked, "Where do you think you're going?"

"To work, of course. Miss Tilly is staying home to bake bread for the poor people whose homes burned down. I'll get her excused at work."

Elizabeth asked, "Where does she work?"

Hallelujah turned and told her, "This is my sister, Mary Jane, and Mary Jane, this is Elizabeth."

A sudden surge of pride and love almost overcame her. Hallelujah felt like weeping for happiness at having a sister like Mary Jane. Never before had she felt like this. She hunched her shoulders to relieve the pain on her back and added: "She works at Armour's Meat Packing Company."

Mary Jane peered around them and said, "I suppose the street car is held up."

Hallelujah began laughing. Elizabeth joined her.

"Held up?" asked Elizabeth. They laughed some more.

"You don't have to go to work, Mary Jane," Elizabeth said. "I watched Armour's burn down from our carriage. It burned in just seven minutes. My papa timed it."

Hallelujah added, "Mr. Joseph's cobbler shop burned down, too. All Chicago downtown is burned. But we have each other, Mary Jane!"

Her voice broke, and overwhelmed with love, she reached to hug her sister. But her hug was as welcome as a muddy puppy jumping on Sunday's best clothes.

Mary Jane held her off with one finger. She patted Hallelujah's scorched sooty shoulder to show that she cared.

"And we have our house." Hallelujah pointed to Elizabeth. "Her house burned down."

Mary Jane brushed ashes off her white blouse. "Are you sure the fire was that bad? I heard about the West Division burning, but not the North Division. They're expecting me at Armour's."

The girls began laughing again.

Mary Jane continued on her way to work.

Chapter Ten

HALLELUJAH COULD HARDLY WAIT TO REACH
home and lie down on her own soft straw bed. The girls
left Mary Jane who insisted on going to her job, and they
continued on their way to the house.

"I'm not even hungry," Hallelujah told Elizabeth. "I'm
just so tired, I want to lie down!"

"Are you sure your mother won't mind?" Elizabeth asked.

"Yes. That's one thing I'm sure of." And as she said it,
Hallelujah's heart seemed to leap in her throat. Miss Tilly
and Mr. Joseph were such good people. They were always
generous to others, and she had never appreciated what
that meant.

As she pulled a hesitant Elizabeth up the front porch
steps, she smelled bread baking. "Smell that," she said.
"Maybe I'm hungry after all."

"Miss Tilly," she called, "I'm home!"

She opened the front door. To her surprise the hall was
full of people lying down. Men and boys were sprawled
under blankets sleeping. An infant began to cry in the

parlor. She jerked the parlor door open, and the room was full of women. A newborn infant lay naked on bloody sheets. Hallelujah shut the door quickly.

They stepped over sleeping bodies and reached the kitchen. Miss Tilly was coming to meet them.

"Honey child!" called Miss Tilly, raising her arms to heaven. "Thank the good Lord!"

Hallelujah began crying. Gratitude and love flooded her. She felt choked with sorrow for all the times she had been mean to Miss Tilly. She could hardly catch her breath. Dirty dress and all, she hugged Miss Tilly, and Miss Tilly buried her in her apron. Finally Hallelujah raised her face and said, "Chicago's burning! Armour's is destroyed, burned down. Elizabeth watched it burn."

She pulled Elizabeth forward. "This is Elizabeth. She's lost from her family, and her house burned down."

Mr. Joseph came in with firewood. "Armour's burned?"

"And your building, Mr. Joseph." She waved her arm dramatically. "All burned down. And our courthouse where President Lincoln lay in state. It burned in twenty minutes." Her back pained, but she couldn't tell Miss Tilly that right now.

"What do you mean, burned?" Mr. Joseph stared at his wife.

Miss Tilly stared back. "One thing the child don't do is tell lies. She might be tricky, but she don't lie outright."

Elizabeth spoke up. "I watched the courthouse burn down." She turned to Hallelujah. "We were together."

Miss Tilly pointed to the sink. "Why don't we have water? Or gaslight? Are the firemen using all the water?"

"Gasworks exploded," said Elizabeth.

"And the waterworks were destroyed," Hallelujah said. "A man said there was a wooden roof over the four pumping engines, and it all burned down." She remembered her brother. "Is Edward Joseph all right?"

Miss Tilly pointed to a corner. The kitchen was warm from the oven and fragrant with the smell of bread baking.

She said, "He just came in. Said he was looking for you in the West Division, and the bridges opened. He couldn't get across to come home. He's plumb tuckered out."

The girls walked into the kitchen to see Edward Joseph sprawled on his back fast asleep on the wooden floor.

"Why is he sleeping there?" Hallelujah asked, her voice shrill from embarrassment. Would Elizabeth think they always slept on the floor? "Why isn't he in his room?"

Miss Tilly looked at her shyly. "It be hard for a child to understand. Your room with Mary Jane, too. Well, you see . . ."

Hallelujah made it easy for her. "You mean people from the fire are sleeping there?" She could hardly believe it.

"Uh, Lord help me," said Miss Tilly. "Yes, honey child. But I tooks your Suzy doll out first." She pointed across the kitchen to show her.

Suzy stood on the kitchen cutting table in the little tan unbleached cotton dress and bonnet Miss Tilly had sewed for her.

Hallelujah laughed aloud. "Suzy!"

She ran to pick up her doll and show Elizabeth. "Here," she said, "you can hold Suzy until you get another French doll."

"I like Suzy," Elizabeth said, and began to hug the doll

and weep. Hallelujah stared at her to make sure she wasn't fooling.

Hallelujah turned back to Miss Tilly who seemed fearful of how she would accept not having her room. "I'm glad you're helping people," Hallelujah said. "There's people everywhere who need help." And she hugged Miss Tilly again.

Mr. Joseph asked, "My shop burned down? Are you sure? Maybe I can save my machinery." He pulled his cap off a peg. "I've got to see for myself."

"Armour's burned down?" Miss Tilly leaned against the stove.

Hallelujah rubbed ashes from her nose. "During the fire," she began, "I walked with Hope . . ."

"God love her!" said Mr. Joseph stepping out the kitchen door. "She walked with hope! Ain't that something now."

"Lord, help us. We all gotta walk with hope!" Miss Tilly said. "But, you children must be starving. Let me feed you!"

For breakfast that morning there were no wheat rolls or corn bread, or pan of eggs, no pork sausages sizzling, no buttery biscuits, no boiled codfish, no hominy grits or oatmeal. There was only hot loaf bread cut for sandwiches to feed the hungry.

After they ate a ham sandwich and drank fresh milk, Hallelujah used a pitch fork to toss straw in the barn. The family had a barn, but they didn't own a horse or carriage.

Sometimes Mr. Post rode one of the livery company horses home for the evening. And he always tended sick horses at home because he could stay with them through the night. The barn was sweet with the smell of fresh cut hay.

Miss Tilly tossed a blanket on the scratchy hay.

"Please look at my back," Hallelujah asked. "I got a burn."

"Poor, honey child," said Miss Tilly. "Let me put some lard on that blister."

Hallelujah twisted her head, but she couldn't see the burn.

Elizabeth said, "It's red and swollen with a big blister in the center. It burned clear through your clothes."

"Well, I'll sleep on my side," Hallelujah said. After Miss Tilly put lard on it, her burn pained more.

Miss Tilly left a sheet to cover the girls. Suzy slept between them, her eyes staring at the pine wood rafters of the barn ceiling.

At noon Hallelujah woke up. As if in a dream, she had heard people talking about water. Miss Tilly's voice was among them.

"Used for the birth . . . water . . ."

"Soup in the pot . . . water . . ."

"Needed for more bread . . . water . . ."

Hallelujah's first thought: I suppose somebody wants me to go for water? Don't they know I'm just a child born into this world through no fault of my own? Why always me? As soon as she recognized how selfishly she had been thinking, she rolled off the hay and grabbed her bonnet. Elizabeth was still sleeping, but Hallelujah had a chance to help.

"Miss Tilly," she called at the kitchen door, "I'll go for water."

"Child, we be needing more water something dreadful."

"I know," she said holding out her hands for buckets.

"Hungry people need that bread. And there's plenty hungry people today. Hungry and homeless."

The kitchen was crowded with people. People from their church, and people from their community, colored and white. The Sullivan wives were there. Never before had Hallelujah seen any of the Irish in their house. The fire certainly was changing how people acted. Behind Hallelujah, Mr. Post came through the door. His face was streaked with rinsed soot.

His first words were, "My company burned. The stables, the livery carriages."

"Lord, no!" said Miss Tilly.

Miss Mary Clare, Patrick Sullivan's wife, said, "The poor horses!"

Mr. Post grinned and raised a fist in triumph. "But not a horse burned! I looked. Someone must have released them. Opened the stalls. Untied the colts!"

"That's good. Now, for water." Hallelujah asked, "Should I go to the river? Or Mr. Steven Hall's well? Or to the lake?"

Mr. Post told her, "The river's clean. The pumps pumping sewage, they burned in the fire. Destroyed like the waterworks, but it makes the river clean. People are down on the riverbanks with buckets and pitchers and cups and glasses.

"Yes, all our horses loosed to save them. But I found my White Star, and she came to my whistle. Rode her all over looking at the fire. It's burning clear north to Lincoln Park," he added sadly.

"The new Lincoln Park be burning?" asked Miss Tilly. "Lord a'mighty!"

"People, hundreds, thousands, standing in the water.

Lill's Brewery burning right on the lake. Coal yards burning.
And here and there a building stands. Fire didn't touch
Saint Patrick's Church on Des Plains Street," he said.

"Is that really true? Oh, it's a miracle!" shouted Miss
Mary Clare. "God saved our church. I must tell Mr. Sullivan." She ran out the door.

Hallelujah stared after her. So their church was saved.
Did that mean that God liked them better than the people
whose churches burned? She wondered about their Provident Baptist Church, and about her school. She even felt
different about school. Now her school was dear to her.

At school she learned grammar, reading, and composi-
tion. She loved reading and writing. The geography and
arithmetic and algebra were all right. But, how she hated
history and the daily Bible reading! Now she might not get
to go to school anymore. Not even to learn history!

Miss Tilly and Mr. Joseph had attended night school to
learn to read and write. When they were children, it was
against the law to teach colored people to read or write, so
they had to learn as adults. It was a privilege, they always
said.

Suddenly, she felt overwhelming love for school. Beeswax! That fire was sure affecting her!

She asked Mr. Post: "School?"

"Burned."

"Provident Baptist?"

"Burned down."

"I'll go for water now," she said abruptly, her throat tight
with hurt. She remembered the child burned to death in
the fire. And the children who lost their mother. So much
pain, so much destroyed. She couldn't grow angry about
her church and her school.

"Honey child," Miss Tilly said, "the river be too far. Run to the lake. Iffen you goes out far enough, the water be pure. And the sand will settle."

"Use your eyes," said Mr. Post. "Dip it clean." He turned to Miss Tilly. "Have you got your basket of food ready?"

As Hallelujah started down the steps, she heard directions. There were relief stations set up. The General Relief Committee had headquarters at the Congregational Church at Washington and Ann streets. People who had food were sharing with people who had none.

Miss Tilly and the Sullivan wives were simmering soup and baking bread for people they were sheltering in their homes. And they were sending baskets of food—ham sandwichs and hot coffee—to relief stations. Church people delivered the baskets.

A train whistle blew. Trains into the unburned South Division were busier than ever.

Hallelujah felt proud to be helping. As she left the yard, she heard Miss Tilly exclaim: "And instead the dear child should be sleeping like Edward Joseph."

Edward Joseph was still sleeping? What about Mary Jane? She wondered if she were back yet. Mary Jane should be working with the women.

Limping from stiffness, her back in fiery pain, she marched toward the lake with a bucket in each hand. I'm strong. I hurt, but I'm strong. I'm not like Elizabeth or Mary Jane or anybody else, and I don't have to be. I'm me. I can help, and I will, she thought.

Chapter Eleven

THE LAKESHORE WAS NOT EMPTY. UNEASY clusters of people huddled in restless groups. The wind blew sandy gusts toward the water, and Hallelujah's mouth and eyes were soon gritty. She tied up her long petticoats and skirt, and took off her shoes and stockings. Wading out, she dipped her buckets in water beyond the line of floating green seaweed. Rough prancing waves soaked her grubby, scorched petticoats and skirt.

Back onshore, she sat on the sand to put on her stockings and shoes, but her shoes were missing. She stared around her, but they weren't there. She yelled into the wind: "Where are my shoes? Somebody stole my new school shoes!"

People looked away from her. She stared at two well-dressed families who were attended by maids and butlers. Other families seemed to be business people, and working people.

She felt angry that no one met her stare. No one came to help her, or to apologize. In fact, no one spoke to her.

She was just a colored girl who came to the lake for water. Others, men and women, were dipping water at the lake, too. And someone among them had stolen her shoes!

Now she was barefoot like the poor children. Like the Sullivans who outgrew their shoes and couldn't afford any more. Like Rachael from the West Division.

Hallelujah yelled and pounded her fists on the shore. Sharp dune grass cut her fingers and made them bleed. Her buckets of water were sprinkled with sand.

"Why would anybody steal from me? Why?" she yelled. "Beeswax, that's mean. Thief! Thief! Thief!"

She yelled so loud her throat ached.

On hands and knees she crawled all around her. Had she misplaced them? No, they were gone. Her stockings were there, her shoes were gone. She sat, face in hands, and began crying.

She was thinking that the thieves let out of jail in the courthouse should have burned in there. Here she was trying to do something good, and someone stole from her. She felt like jerking bundles from people nearby and searching them for her shoes, her pretty brown leather shoes.

Suddenly she asked herself: How important are shoes? Since Mr. Joseph didn't have a shoemaking business any more, she might never have nice brown shoes again. That was scary.

Then she raised her face to the hazy smoke-filled sky, and thought: Children lost their mothers in the fire. Elizabeth lost her home. People were moaning with horrible burns. A great fire had burned down Chicago, and she was crying over a mere pair of shoes?

She was still Hallelujah with or without shoes.

Going home her feet were tender because she wasn't used to going barefoot. Sand at the shore felt sharp and cold. Prickly pine cones and sharp dune grass cut and bruised her feet, and yet she enjoyed feeling with wiggling toes. Wet petticoats and skirt made her legs cold in the wind. Beyond the lakeshore, warm dust squeezed through her toes, and dry leaves popped and crackled as she shuffled through them.

Maybe those poor children enjoyed going barefoot?

Close to her house, she gazed at it. Never had the house seemed more beautiful. At every window Miss Tilly had fluffy white curtains.

She bumped the pickets of the fence as she passed. Dear old wooden fence. Elizabeth was still sleeping in the barn. Dear old barn. Setting a bucket on the steps, she pulled open the kitchen door.

Her beloved warm kitchen was filled with the good smells of food; it was also filled with ladies and gentlemen from church. To be honest, she was tired of so many people in her house.

"And blankets if you have any extra," someone called.

She wanted to yell, Don't give away our blankets! We'll never see them again; but she bit her tongue. People were chilly. People needed blankets. They could share.

"Here's the water," a neighbor said, and several women rushed to her with saucepans to dip in her buckets.

No one remarked about the clean water. About how such a small child could carry two buckets of heavy water. In fact, no one seemed to appreciate how good she was being. Beeswax! She reached in a basket and took a sandwich for herself and one for Elizabeth, then she turned and started down the steps.

But Miss Tilly saw her and ran through the crowd in the kitchen. She kissed Hallelujah's forehead as they hugged on the steps. "You be so good. Ain't like the same child. Thank you, honey child. Now go feed your friend."

Dear Miss Tilly! Hallelujah felt a little better, but Miss Tilly still hadn't asked about her blister or noticed her bare bleeding feet! She shook her head at how she was thinking. Remember, she told herself, you're a strong-hearted girl!

The next time Hallelujah woke up, she and Elizabeth both offered to walk to the lake for water. However, Elizabeth asked for warm water from the stove to wash her face and hands first.

While her friend was washing up, Hallelujah threaded her way over legs and necks of men sprawled and sleeping in the hall. Upstairs in her room a Polish family of six children slept around their mother. One girl was Hallelujah's size, but probably younger. Their mother was nursing a plump little boy. She smiled apologetically at Hallelujah.

Hallelujah forced a smile. "Make yourself at home," she said. The lady answered in Polish in a low voice.

In the corner wardrobe cabinet Mary Jane had a pair of black shoes she'd outgrown. The leather was stiff but Hallelujah plopped on the floor and tried them on. As she suspected, the shoes were too long. She had a plan for that.

From her pocket, she pulled hay brought from the barn. When hay was stuffed in each toe, she packed it solid. The next time she tried on the shoes, they fit. No more cut feet.

With protective shoes on Hallelujah and a rinsed face on Elizabeth, the girls trotted off for the lake. At the shore, Hallelujah set Elizabeth to guard her shoes. Hallelujah

waded out and filled two buckets for herself, and one for
Elizabeth.

To save hot water, Hallelujah washed her face and neck
and arms and hands in the cold lake waters. She was being
so considerate the goodness was killing her. She used cold
water, but Elizabeth had asked for warm. She let cold water
drip on her blister, and it felt better. If only she could hold
cold water on it.

New families rested on the shore. She asked, but none
of them had seen her shoes.

"That's terrible for someone to steal your shoes," said
Elizabeth, as they headed home.

"I know. There are some mean people in this world."
Hallelujah thought about herself, how mean she sometimes
acted.

"I was mean," Elizabeth said in a low voice. "I wouldn't
let you hold my Betsy doll. And you and your family have
been so kind to me."

Hallelujah shook her head. Elizabeth was still feeling
guilty about the silly doll. For all they knew, Elizabeth's
parents might have burned in the fire, but Hallelujah didn't
mention it. Hardly able to walk, Elizabeth rested her bucket
on the sand. With a sigh, she rubbed her arm.

Hallelujah waited.

Elizabeth said, "You know what I was thinking when I
wouldn't let you hold Betsy? I didn't want you to dirty her.
Wasn't that silly? Your color doesn't wash off."

Hallelujah said, "Now you're eating our food and sleeping
in our barn. What about that?"

After they began walking again, Hallelujah asked: "Do
you think you're different from me?"

In a trembling voice Elizabeth said, "We're both children. We have the same feelings and needs. Our houses are different, but like you said, all kinds of houses burned before that wind and fire."

Hallelujah nodded. "There's a little girl upstairs. She's our size, and she's Polish. Their family is living with us now, and a week from now they may not speak to us on the street. White people who work with Miss Tilly and talk all day at Armour's, wouldn't be caught dead speaking to her on the street."

"Oh, Hallelujah," said Elizabeth loudly, "I know better now. I'll never treat poor people mean, not even our servants. I made a promise."

"You did? Who did you promise?"

Elizabeth seemed surprised at the question. She rested her bucket again. Hallelujah impatiently set down her buckets. This trip was taking forever because Elizabeth was so slow.

"I just promised, that's all."

"You can't promise without promising someone."

"I promised God," Elizabeth said shyly.

"Oh, that's different. Did you make a deal with God?"

"What do you mean?"

"I mean, you promise to do something for God, if God will do something for you?"

Elizabeth seemed horrified. "Oh, no!"

"That's even better. I think I'll make a promise, too." Hallelujah was impressed. Thinking furiously, she began to walk faster. If Elizabeth could make a promise, so could she!

Elizabeth called for her to wait.

Hallelujah wondered: How had Elizabeth made that promise? Had she shouted and raised both arms as people in church did when they repented sin and promised to live a good life? Beeswax, she bet not! Elizabeth had probably whispered, eyes squinted closed, hands folded primly. Well, Hallelujah would do better than that!

That Monday night at the house on State Street, Mr. Post asked Elizabeth about her parents. He took their names and addresses.

"There's an Intelligence Office," he said. "Lost people are reporting names there. You can ask about families and friends. You should see the place. It's mobbed."

That's smart, Hallelujah thought. People are organized!

When she had reached home that morning, she had been happy to escape to a clear clean street. Now she was itching to see the burning city again. Someone bumped the door. She turned.

Mr. Joseph pulled himself through the kitchen doorway. He shuffled over to the wooden rocker, and lowered himself slowly. He shook his head. He seemed about to speak several times, but he was choked up. Finally, head in hands, he wept.

Miss Tilly hurried to hug his head against her skirt.

Frantically, Hallelujah glanced around. Never had Mr. Joseph cried before. Luckily, the church people and neighbors were gone. Only family, Mr. Post, and Elizabeth were there.

The Polish baby upstairs was wailing, and the newborn in the parlor began to fret. Mary Jane walked into the kitchen and sensing the trouble, quickly closed the door. She leaned against it with a frightened stare.

With a big sob, Mr. Joseph raised his head. He said, "The city of Chicago is dead. The fire has burned to the city limits. Clear to Fullerton Avenue. We'll probably starve this winter. It's all over."

No, no, thought Hallelujah. That can't be true! Isn't there always hope? Or was that a joke that a "parrot" would repeat? Walking with Hope. She was afraid to speak, after all, what did she know? She was only a child. And Mr. Joseph was struggling to stop crying long enough to tell them more.

Chapter Twelve

MR. JOSEPH BEGAN: "THE BANKS AND INSUR-
ance companies burned down. There's no money left. My
business was insured, but it don't mean nothing now." He
shuddered.

"I watched them pull out a bank vault," he said. "Wasn't
melted. Got it open. All the money was nothing but blackened ashes. Money? Ashes blew away in the wind." He
went on, "My shoemaking shop? All the iron and steel
machines? Twisted and melted. Glass windows? Bubbled
into melted drops. Fire burned over four miles long and a
mile wide. Heart of the city is blasted into burning ash. It's
like the child said, but I still can't believe it."

Miss Tilly began to rock back and forth moaning. Hallelujah remembered whenever she was sick with a high
fever, Miss Tilly rocked and moaned. All the old colored
people did it. "Oh, Jesus, save us!" whispered Miss Tilly.

For a long time no one moved. No one spoke. Mr. Post
gave a deep shuddering sigh and said, "They're saying the
business will go to Cincinnati now. St. Louis will prosper.

Yes, indeed, Cincinnati and St. Louis will take the place of Chicago. And, New York, of course.

"They're saying Chicago is dead," Mr. Post added, "Queen of the Prairies they used to call her. Now she's gone. All the business sections wiped out in the fire. A hundred thousand people without homes. That's about a third of the people living in Chicago, and winter coming! All the millionaires wiped out."

Mr. Joseph said, "And, they're the people built this city up, let's remember that! Millionaires got their money in the War Between the States, and built this city up. But it's all gone now."

"Chicago. Queen of the West," said Mr. Post, sniffing.

In the face of men crying and such deep despair, Hallelujah was afraid to speak. Elizabeth had begun to cry; Mary Jane was crying; Miss Tilly was crying. Miss Tilly's brown face had tears flowing, and she hadn't wiped at them. Kneeling beside the rocker, her hands were busy stroking her husband's shoulders, and she rocked on her knees and moaned.

Hallelujah felt like rocking and moaning herself, but she didn't moan, and she didn't cry. She wanted to say something, but she didn't want to repeat other people.

Tomorrow there was no school to go to.

Sunday there would be no church to go to.

Elizabeth had no home to go to.

Mr. Joseph, Miss Tilly, Mary Jane, and Edward Joseph had no work to go to.

Hallelujah spied Suzy Dollperson, and inched toward her.

She picked up her doll. She began thinking that Suzy was a nice name, and she wouldn't ever change her name.

But, if she ever got another doll, she sure knew what she would name it.

Miss Tilly waved her toward the door. Grown-ups wanted to talk. She and Elizabeth would have to sleep on the hay again. For nap time, it had been like an adventure. But, she didn't look forward to a night out there with owls and rabbits and rats.

Hugging Suzy so tightly the wood hurt her ribs, Hallelujah pulled Elizabeth toward the door. Her friend hesitated, too.

Babies cried. They heard rapid Polish spoken. Strangers from the fire. The very house seemed alive with creaking boards and muffled conversations. Hallelujah wished the people would all disappear, and things would be back to normal. But, she understood, she must be considerate.

Just as they reached the kitchen door, it sprang open. Mr. Patrick Sullivan and his brother Cornelius stood in the doorway with hunting guns in their hands.

Elizabeth gave a frightened cry.

The brothers politely tipped their caps, and slipped into the warm hushed kitchen.

Mr. Patrick said, "They need men to patrol the city."

His brother added, "There's looters all over. People setting more fires. People robbing the homeless as they stand by all they own in this world!"

"It's crazy," said Mr. Patrick Sullivan. "Seems people arriving free are taking advantage of us. Not only that. Since the trains are free, people are fleeing this city like rats off a sinking ship."

Mr. Joseph stood. "I'll volunteer. I couldn't sleep anyway." He lifted his rifle off the kitchen wall pegs.

Mr. Post said, "Come back about one o'clock, Mr. LaSalle. I'll sleep now and take a second shift for you."

The girls turned and left to sleep in the barn.

From the barn Hallelujah and Elizabeth heard neighborhood men gathering on State Street in front of their house. To the north and west fires still burned, that Monday night of October 9, 1871, lighting the night sky with a horrible yellow color. And still the wind blew.

On Tuesday morning the constant smell of burning made Hallelujah more angry than she could ever remember feeling.

"I don't know what we'll do," she told Elizabeth as they ate breakfast in the kitchen.

Miss Tilly had fried green sausage and cooked hominy grits special for them. Their milk was creamy and cool.

"Can't you visit relatives?" Elizabeth asked.

Hallelujah thought, What relatives? "I don't know any. Our church people are like family, but we're all in the same boat. I mean fire."

"I'm sure we'll go somewhere else," Elizabeth said between bites of sausage. "Possibly Paris."

Sure, thought Hallelujah, flee Chicago like the rats! Rats off the sinking boat, the boat they were all in together. The fire they were all in together. Or something like that.

She suddenly hated her new friend. However, in spite of her feelings, she tried hard to be patient with her. The fire had changed her, all that fire couldn't be in vain.

"Hold Suzy," she asked her quickly. "There's Mr. Post."

Sooty from a night in wind and ashes, he stood in the kitchen doorway. "I'll take one load of sandwiches to the

relief station," he told Miss Tilly. "Then I'll sleep." He
stepped out of the kitchen.

Outside, Hallelujah clutched his arm. In a deep whisper
she asked, "Please, I have to go with you. Please, Mr. Post."

"Well," he said smiling at her expression, "Edward Joseph
been delivering with me. He runs the food in."

"I'll do it, honest. I'll do it. I've been hauling water."

"Your mama been telling me."

"I have to go back. Please?"

"Did you lose something in the fire?"

"No, but I have to do something back at the fire."

He shook his head sadly. "The fire's no place for a child."

She stepped back. "They always say that to children. So
maybe I'm not a child anymore."

"No," he said patting her back. She jumped because her
blister still pained. "Stay a child," he said. "Enjoy being a
child while you can. I'll see what Miss Tilly say."

After all the work Hallelujah had done, how could Miss
Tilly refuse? Besides, Hallelujah was a hard child to tell
no. Miss Tilly said, "But, honey child, you be leaving your
little guest."

"That's all right," Elizabeth said quietly.

"She says it's all right," Hallelujah said. "And there's
something I have to do back there."

Miss Tilly raised a warning finger. "Obey Mr. Post. Don't
you leave sight of him at no time never!"

On White Star, Hallelujah rode sidesaddle behind Mr.
Post.

They delivered sandwiches and coffee to a relief station
in the South Division. Women and men were receiving

food at a church, and carrying it out to the prairie where families had fled from the fire. Thousands sat in the grassy prairie with bundles saved from the fire.

"Thank you kindly," said a large woman with big red hands. "The workmen will be hungry tonight."

"Workmen?" Hallelujah asked Mr. Post. What a strange word for the lady to use. "Who's working now?"

"Well, you know, it's a manner of speaking."

"Please," she said, "I know you're tired from patrolling all night. But ride through a little of the fire."

"Still burning and it's the third day: Sunday, Monday, Tuesday."

"I know," she said.

"Daresay some of them Chicago coal yards be burning for weeks. But, might not be nobody here to see."

"Are you leaving, too?" Hallelujah asked.

"Don't know. Where'd I go?"

The closer they rode to the burned area, the more the stench of smoke and burned flesh increased. It filled Hallelujah with deep sadness.

As they rode, besides the howling wind, there were new sounds. Sounds of chipping brick, sounds of hammers.

When they turned around a brick chimney still standing, they saw dozens of men with trowels chipping away at white mortar stuck on red bricks. Hallelujah couldn't understand at all. Other men and women were milling about in the smoky rubble tossing hot bricks onto cleared lots.

Cleared lots?

Dozens of children and adults were shoveling ashes and rolling ash away in wheelbarrows. They had cleared lots.

Mr. Post stopped White Star and stared.

Hallelujah remembered her promise not to leave him, but curiosity overcame her. She slid to the smoking street, and ran over to a group of colored men with trowels and bricks.

"What are you doing?" she yelled.

The first man smiled at her. "We're buiding Chicago again," he said. "Come help. Plenty work for children."

"Post!" called a Teuton. "Over here."

Mr. Post rode near cautiously. He was not giving up his horse, or being taken advantage of, either.

"Have you got a wheelbarrow?" the man asked.

Mr. Post nodded yes.

"Bring it. We're rebuilding the city. Bigger and better than ever. We need everyone."

Now Hallelujah understood that people were cleaning bricks to use again. After they were cleaned, children collected them and built orderly stacks. She ran to Mr. Post and he pulled her back up on White Star.

They rode along Washington Street. They turned corners and everywhere they saw feverish activity. No one was sitting in sad teary groups anymore; everyone was busy working.

"Oh, my God," said Mr. Post, "they must be crazy!"

Chapter Thirteen

MR. POST SEEMED WORRIED ABOUT WHAT THEY saw before them; Hallelujah shivered, but she had a mission.

"Please, Mr. Post, ride to LaSalle Street."

He tapped White Star. In a scary whisper he said, "If I didn't drive a livery cab, I wouldn't know where I was. Can't tell one street from another. All burned. No buildings to act as landmarks. I'm counting corners."

They passed a pile of burned bodies waiting to be buried. Large and small, even an infant, the bodies were blackened so that Hallelujah couldn't tell who they were. Some bodies were her size, children for sure.

The fire had destroyed a city, had killed people. She closed her eyes and trembled. All this destruction. All this suffering. Her small blister hurt so much. But many people were burned all over their bodies, much worse than she was. She grew dizzy and sick to her stomach. To keep from falling, she held Mr. Post's coattails tightly. She opened her eyes.

Block after city block, sooty people were busy working

everywhere. Men rolled wheelbarrows filled with ashes, women dragged crates filled with ashes, children hauled wicker baskets filled with ashes.

Hallelujah called, "Where are you taking the ashes?"

"To the lake," a woman answered. "Come help."

"The lake?"

"We'll build up ground out there," a man shouted. "Extend the city. It's all right, you know. They told us to do it. They're paying us."

"Paying them?" asked Mr. Post. "Who has money?"

A white-haired man passed on horseback. Hearing Mr. Post, he rode closer. " 'Twas a colored man what helped save our city," he said, hooking thumb in vest. "You coloreds should be proud."

"Saved the city?" asked Mr. Post.

The man rode on without saying anything else. Mr. Post whispered, "Who told them? What are they doing?"

"Mr. Post," said Hallelujah sliding off White Star, "I'm going right by the courthouse. I have to."

He nodded sadly. "I'm going looking for my boss. See if I can find a carriage to run delivery. Stay there till I come back."

She ran as fast as she could. Bankers on LaSalle Street had men digging furiously through ashes. She ran past jewelry boxes and silverware abandoned and dumped in the street.

At State and Randolph a pretty young woman stood among ashes selling red apples from a crate. Hallelujah thought, Good! Chicago would live again for sure, and this lady knew it. She could hardly wait to get back and tell Mr. Joseph.

She ran to the spot where she and Elizabeth had stood watching the courthouse cupola tumble in flames. Once buildings had stood five and seven stories high along there. Now it was a smoking wasteland; it was flattened to a prairie of ash and rubble. The sight was terrible and awesome at the same time.

Some places a piece of wall or chimney stood where a building had been. In just one night, all that destruction. She rubbed her eyes expecting it to change back any minute, but it didn't. She looked around her. The frantically working people were too busy to notice. She waited until a wagon passed.

Then she raised both arms dramatically toward the sky.

She was pleased that the wind still howled noisily, so that workers couldn't hear her. Turning her back, she felt pelting ash on her skirt.

Arms high, she called: "Lord God, listen to me. I'm Hallelujah, born on Easter Sunday morning. You know how I used to be mean to people. Well, I'm sorry now. I think differently. I know it's all right to be an orphan, and a Mississippi slave child. This is who I am. So now I want to be helpful and kind. I promise to be good. Help me to keep my promise, Lord God Almighty!"

Pleased with herself, she lowered her arms and looked around again. Only one boy watched her. The boy waved, smiled, and lifted another shovel of ash. She felt a little embarrassed, but she felt proud.

She only hoped she had done it right, her promise to God. She bet Elizabeth hadn't made her promise in a special place with arms raised. Hallelujah bet she made the best promise ever, but now she had to keep it. That would be the hard part.

Slowly she walked all around the courthouse square. She saw twisted telegraph cables. She saw metal beams bent and melted out of shape. Safety boxes and pieces of smoking wood from furniture littered the streets. Some wandering women and children picked through the ashes.

Nothing interested Hallelujah until she spotted a metal teapot with a curved handle and long spout. She saw lilies carved on the gray metal. Quickly she hugged it to her. Miss Tilly might like that. She loved tea.

Balls of melted glass had crazy designs in them. She gathered some. She became so busy Mr. Post had to yell to her. He had succeeded in obtaining a carriage and had White Star harnessed to it.

She ran to climb up onto the carriage.

As they rode, another carriage passed. The man driving stared at her lap. "What have you got there, colored girl?" he asked.

"Melted glass, sir." Only little fist-size balls of melted glass. She held them out.

His wife was dressed in a blue serge jacket and skirt. "What nice souvenirs," she said "Buy them, Horace."

The man reached into his pocket. "How much?"

"How many do you want?" Hallelujah called above the wind.

"Oh, say five."

"Five dollars," she said boldly. Mr. Post was startled. That was a lot of money. After all, he paid only three dollars a week in room and board.

The man handed her five dollars and drove on.

"Hurry," Hallelujah told Mr. Post. "We have so much to tell them at home!"

Back at their house she ran in the front door. Men and boys were no longer sleeping in the hall, but voices came from the parlor. The dining room was full of people who sounded excited.

In the kitchen Mr. Patrick Sullivan stood grinning. His red hair stood high in flamelike tufts because he kept rubbing his head.

"Jobs!" he was shouting. "They're paying twenty-five dollars a week!"

"Twenty-five dollars a week? I can't believe it," said Miss Tilly from her rocker by the stove. Ten dollars a week was good pay for a man.

Mr. Post strode in from the back door. "It's true. People working everywhere. Men. Women. Children. Clearing ash to the lake. Gonna build up more land for the city out there. Cleaning bricks to rebuild. Knocking off the mortar. And they say they're being paid. We're building Chicago, bigger and better than ever!" He shook his head in wonder.

Everyone shook hands. Mr. Joseph kissed Miss Tilly and whirled her around. She looked embarrassed but pleased.

Hallelujah jumped up and down and hugged Mr. Joseph. She was so happy for him! With money he could buy leather and machines for a new shoemaker shop.

She would have new shoes again. Mary Jane's old shoes hurt her feet. And people with jobs could buy shoes. Mr. Joseph would smell like good leather and shoe wax again!

Mr. Cornelius Sullivan spoke up. "Edward Joseph, bring a brush and some paint. They're paying three dollars a sign.

Signs springing up like corn in the springtime. Bank doing business at a church. Hardware store over in a West Division warehouse. Got to tell folks where to do business, you know."

Edward Joseph ran out the door for paint. Hallelujah hid her metal teapot in a corner and ran after him.

"Say," she said, "I'm sorry, you know. But look what I got." She showed him five clean dollar bills.

"Where'd you get them?" he asked, reaching out his hand.

"I'm selling souvenirs from the fire." She jerked the five dollars back from him. "I also got a burn on my back. It's big and red and blistered. But it's better now. And I can make money. Wait until I tell my friends!"

"Oh, great!" Edward Joseph said. He touched her cheek. "Yeah, I'm sorry, too. Bye now. I'm going to paint signs."

She returned to the kitchen. Everyone was gleeful and noisy except for Elizabeth. She was holding Suzy on her lap, sitting on a stool cutting carrots. She was slow and clumsy with the knife. Pieces of carrot were in chips all over the kitchen floor. Hallelujah ran over and hugged her.

"Isn't it wonderful?" she asked.

Mr. Post waved a paper. "Your name is at the Intelligence Office," he told Elizabeth. "And people know where you are at this address. They'll be here soon, I'm sure."

Elizabeth smiled weakly. "Thank you," she said.

Hallelujah picked up the teapot from the corner and ran to Miss Tilly. "Here," she said, offering the sooty teapot. "I found this. Nobody claimed it, so it's yours."

"Oh, my," said Miss Tilly. "What a fine metal pot." She flipped back the pointed top, and peeked inside.

"It's silver," said Elizabeth. "My mother has two silver tea services with teapots like that."

Miss Tilly held it out. "Is this your mama's?"

"Oh, no."

"A silver teapot. Oh, my." Miss Tilly looked as pleased as a cat over a glass of spilled milk. Her fingers traced the lilies and their long thin leaves. She smiled at the girls.

Dressed in Hallelujah's unbleached cotton school dress, Elizabeth looked like one of the neighborhood children. She sucked a cut finger. Hallelujah nudged her.

"Come on," she told Elizabeth. "We have to call my friends. Hurry!"

Chapter Fourteen

THE SKY WAS SMOKY GRAY FROM CLOUDS CAR-
rying ash. Grit swirled in circles over the grass, bleached
yellow from dryness. The air was chilly, and the wind off
the southwest prairie continued to howl.

Hallelujah dragged Elizabeth to homes around her neighborhood and called her friends.

"There's work for children rebuilding Chicago," she said.
"Signs to paint, bricks to pile up, souvenirs to sell."

The crowd of brown faces grew excited. Children ran off
quickly to ask permission to go to the fire. "We'll meet you
there," Timothy called. Mary Sue waved.

Several bigger children laughed aloud. At last they
could make money. They didn't even have to skip going to
school, because there were no schools to attend. Somehow
Hallelujah knew she wouldn't see her friends for a long
time.

Liza and Beth Ann left her, too. Liza called: "Mama may
have and Papa may have, but God bless the child that's
got its own!"

Hallelujah told Elizabeth, "Folks always say that when children are busy doing good for themselves."

Elizabeth listened and stared at Hallelujah's friends.

Rheba stayed with them. "My folks be too busy to care," she said. "Hallelujah, I'se with you."

Next Hallelujah gathered the Sullivan children from next door. Maura, Patrick, and Daniel Sullivan sat with her, Elizabeth, and Rheba on hay in the barn. The barn was warm, fragrant of sweet hay, and out of the chilly gusts of air.

"We'll use baskets to gather these glass balls," she told them. "We call out, 'Souvenir of the fire, souvenir!' "

"What's a souvenir?" Daniel asked.

Hallelujah shrugged. "Look, what does it matter? A lady paid for them and called them souvenirs. That's good enough for me."

"I ain't calling no word I don't know what means," Rheba said. Rheba and Hallelujah were the same age.

Elizabeth said, "We buy souvenirs from every city we visit in Europe and the East. I think it means, something to remember the city by."

"Sure," Maura said. "Souvenir of the fire. I've heard of souvenirs. But will my mama like me selling things?"

Daniel said, "I bet not."

"Won't catch *me* out there calling 'souvenir,' " Patrick said.

"Sorry, Hallelujah," said Maura, taking Daniel's hand. "Thanks for telling us."

Rheba said, "Let 'em white children go. Us going to sell souvenirs!"

Hallelujah frowned at her. Rheba never felt comfortable

around white people, but Hallelujah knew the Sullivans as neighbors and friends. She wanted them along.

"Sure, go ahead," Hallelujah called. "Too proud to work to help your family, huh?" Her voice rose higher.

They had slid off the hay and trotted hand in hand over to the barn door. A gust of grit blew in the door.

"But you can steal in the dark of night!" she added.

Maura stopped. Patrick jerked her forward. Daniel looked up to Maura.

Hallelujah shouted: "Your mama sends you to steal coal off the tracks. You steal wood, too, in the winter!"

Like an angry bobcat, Maura turned and shouted: "That's different. Your papa has a business. Our papas are working men!"

"And you don't want to work and help them?" Hallelujah called.

"We're Irish," Patrick said. "We don't beg."

"No, you'll starve before you'll beg," Hallelujah said, and something stuck in her throat. She remembered carrying the pots of food to them. It embarrassed them so much they couldn't even acknowledge the food. And she had promised she wouldn't hurt people or be mean to them.

In a softer voice, she said, "Know what they paid me?"

Maura turned to find out, but Patrick yanked on her hand to leave. "I'm sorry, Hallelujah," she said, "but . . ."

"Well," said Hallelujah, "all I know is that my sister Mary Jane works all week long for four dollars and fifty cents and hides the fifty cents. That's a week's pay for a working girl. But I got even more than that."

"You did?" asked Maura. Her voice was squeaky with surprise.

"Come on," said Patrick. "They're coloreds. As slaves they used to be worked like mules, and get beat when they stopped. They don't know nothing. We're Irish."

Rheba balled her fists and showed her teeth. She yelled, "Kill 'em!" Hallelujah pushed Rheba to sit back down on the hay.

"Five dollars in green color," Hallelujah said softly, "and money in my colored hand is the same as money in your white hand. We mighta been born into this world with different color skins, but we still got the same kinda bodies under them skins. Same bodies and the same color blood in our hearts."

Her words seemed to hiss, and breathlessness showed how angry she was. She couldn't forget that she helped feed these Sullivans.

Maura said, "Five dollars? I don't believe you."

Hallelujah pulled the cash from her pocket and spread it in a wicked fan like gambling cards. "Your mama don't have to know about it."

Elizabeth said, "Five dollars? Really? My maid only gets three dollars a week. Of course, she lives with us and eats at our house for free."

Hallelujah waved the money. Patrick and Daniel stared as if she were waving a snake. They seemed hypnotized.

"Next week they'll make us go back to school," said Hallelujah. "We children born into this world through no fault of our own only have a little time. All these rich people are coming to see our Chicago fire. They want souvenirs, but they don't want to get dirty."

The Sullivan cousins stood in a timid row clasping hands like cutout paper dolls. Daniel seemed to be trembling.

Maura began to smile. "We wouldn't have to tell them. Mama asked us to see what we could pick up from the fire. My uncle found a gold watch that still kept time and a chest full of fine silverware."

"My father would call it enterprising," Elizabeth told them.

"So, what does that mean?" Hallelujah looked disgusted.

"I'm not too sure," she said, "but it's like good business."

"See there," said Hallelujah, "we're enterprising! We're a souvenir selling business. Who's with me?"

Rheba's hand went up. "Us needs the money! Us ain't too proud."

"Is it work?" Patrick asked. "Because we're workingmen."

Maura dropped the boys' hands. "Yes, we'll do it."

"Sure," Hallelujah said, "you work finding them and wiping them clean. We'll sell them."

Daniel asked, "Can I be a workingman, too?" He scratched his leg and grinned. At last they all agreed.

"We're in business, a working business," Hallelujah corrected quickly. These Sullivans were sensitive about which class of society they were in. She raised her arms in triumph.

Elizabeth said, "Maybe you shouldn't tell until you make more money."

"You?" asked Hallelujah, "isn't it 'we'? Aren't you helping?"

"Oh, yes," Elizabeth said stiffly.

"See there!" Hallelujah said.

Daniel was jumping up and down. "I'll get a bushel basket."

"Me, too," called Patrick.

Elizabeth pointed to a rough pine board. "Is that important?" She stood up.

"It's supposed to go with the firewood," Hallelujah said.

"We need a sign," said Elizabeth. "Find me some paint and I'll paint a sign on there." She picked up the board.

"Will whitewash do?" asked Maura, backing toward the door.

Elizabeth wrinkled her nose. "I suppose so."

"Now," said Hallelujah, hands on hips, "I want you all to meet back here as soon as you can. Bring baskets, wiping cloths, a jug for water, a cigar box for the money . . ."

"We'll split the money four ways," Maura called. "The Sullivans, the LaSalles, Elizabeth, and Rheba."

"No," said Hallelujah. "There are more of you working. We divvy up equally."

"Quick, the paint," Elizabeth said.

Business for the children on LaSalle Street in the burned district of Chicago was brisk. They set up a blackened barrel and leaned the sign Elizabeth painted against it. Her sign read SOUVENIRS OF THE GREAT CHICAGO FIRE!

Patrick and Daniel ran about finding molten glass balls in cracked designs and colors. A nearby church had lost its stained glass windows, and the boys found lovely colored glass there.

Patrick found twisted pieces of metal. "Ain't they pretty?"

"We're selling glass," Maura told him. "Can't you tell metal from glass?"

A lady with an ostrich feather in her bonnet leaned out of her carriage. "May I see the delightful artwork?" she asked. She pointed to the metal piece in Patrick's hand.

Hallelujah grabbed it and wiped it clean. "Art souvenir from the Great Chicago Fire!" she called. "Seven dollars."

"I'll take it."

Elizabeth wrapped it in newspaper and laid it on the lady's gloved palm.

After the lady left, Elizabeth leaned over the basket. She asked, "Can I save that one for my papa? And that one. He'll use them as paperweights. These really are nice."

"That's twelve dollars," Hallelujah said, counting the balls she pointed to.

"He'll pay."

"You can pay," Maura said. "Look how much money we have!"

"Hey, you ragamuffins," a rough-looking man called. "What are you doing there?"

He wore a dusty brown derby and a soiled brown suit. Something about him reminded Hallelujah of the prisoners released from the jail Sunday night.

Elizabeth stepped back, and the Sullivans glanced from one to another, but Hallelujah walked toward him. "Yes, sir," she said boldly. "What would you like?"

Chapter Fifteen

AS HALLELUJAH STEPPED CLOSER TO THE MAN, she knew she had seen him before. He really had been a prisoner in the courthouse basement. He strode over to their baskets and peeked in.

"Selling glass and little bitty pieces of metal is fine, but no big pieces. You hear?"

"No, sir," Maura said meekly.

Hallelujah wondered why. What was this outlaw up to now? "Why not, sir? What are you going to do with metal?" she asked.

He grinned and a tooth was missing in the front. He opened his coat and stuck his thumbs in his suspenders. His white shirt was filthy with sooty handprints on the front.

"I'm in the metal salvage business," he said. "We're digging for water pipes, gas pipes, metal safes, scales—whatever we can find. Any stoves, mantels, columns made of metal. We even found some twisted chandeliers."

Hallelujah wondered what chandeliers were.

"And we'll haul them to the foundry. Gonna melt them down and use them to rebuild Chicago. This here city is gonna be greater than it's ever been!"

His red tongue showed through the gap in his teeth, like raw meat at the market. It was sickening to Hallelujah, but she reminded herself that he was a human being, and that he had set himself up in business just as they had.

Patrick pointed. "Over there's a big chunk. Can't tell what is was, but it's metal."

"That's fine," said the man. "Any big metal you can show me, I'll pay you fifty cents."

Patrick held out his hand. "I'll take my fifty cents and show you." They walked off together.

Hallelujah watched them carefully. She still didn't trust the man. She told Maura, "For someone who didn't want to work, your cousin is doing fine."

"What chandeliers be?"' asked Rheba.

Hallelujah and the Sullivans didn't know either.

Elizabeth opened her arms to show the size. "They hang from chains and hold candles and little glass pieces. The light dances around off the glass."

"I wonder where he found the chandelier?" Maura asked. "The glass must be nice."

Daniel returned with a full bushel. "Here's more money," he said. "A man bought some balls before I even got to wipe them."

"What's that?" Elizabeth asked, pointing down the street.

"Where?" Hallelujah asked.

Elizabeth pointed to two dozen men in trousers and suspenders with caps on their heads. They were marching vigorously in step along the middle of the street. Someone among them was yelling. As they passed, some men cleaning bricks stood up and joined them.

"I wonder what they're gonna do?" Maura said.

"They're Germans, Teutons," Patrick said. He had returned safely with fifty cents. "My papa says the Teutons run this city. They get the jobs first."

"That's because there are more of them," said Maura.

As they passed, Hallelujah called to them. "Bitte, please, where are you going?"

Most of them strode solemnly forward. There was a spring to their steps. Caps were tipped forward over eyes, shoulders were squared and proud.

"Where are you going? What are you gonna do?" Hallelujah ran after them and boldly tugged on a young man's jacket.

He grinned at her. "We've been hired," he said proudly. "They got a load of lumber rolled into the South Division. We're clearing basements."

Hallelujah put her hands on her hips. "What's lumber got to do with basements?"

The young German shrugged and ran to catch up with the group of marching workmen.

"Souvenirs!" the children called as a carriage rode past. A lady smiled but passed by. Families from Wisconsin and Indiana were visiting Chicago to sightsee. They came free on the trains, and hired livery carriages. Mr. Post had been quite busy.

Patrick and Daniel returned with more glass balls.

"Tell you one thing," Patrick said. "Everything didn't

burn in this fire. There's wagons over there full of molasses and vinegar and flour in barrels."

"Soap and brooms and mops," Daniel added.

"People are ready to sell," said Patrick.

"Business," Hallelujah said laughing. "Chicago's in business again, and the fire's still burning in the North Division!"

Rheba said, "It be burning here, too." She stamped out some glowing cinders on the street.

Within hours gangs of men cleared stone basements of ash and smoking rubble. Then wagons of fresh pine pulled by work horses clunk-clunked on the street. And the clatter of hammers began.

"I love that smell," Hallelujah said. "That fresh pinewood smell." Their souvenir stand was near the construction work.

"Me too," said Maura. "Especially since it means pay for workingmen."

"And people with pay can buy shoes from my papa,'" Hallelujah said. She turned to Elizabeth. "What does your papa do?"

Elizabeth held a glass ball high to the light. "My papa is in surveying and architecture. He's built commercial buildings all over the world."

"Oh," said Maura, "then he's a carpenter."

"No."

"A brick mason?" asked Hallelujah.

"No, he designs buildings. Tells people how to build them."

Hallelujah said, "Mr. Joseph told Edward Joseph how to build a bird house once."

Before they left downtown Chicago that Tuesday evening, there were several new stores. They were little more than basements with fresh pinewood walls and slanted wooden roofs. Sign painters printed right on the pine walls.

Elizabeth said, "That's terribly ugly."

"It be roofs over they heads," Rheba said as they walked.

A man riding a horse passed them and commented: "This slabtown is the beginning of commerce in a new Chicago!"

The children cheered and danced in little steps.

They walked home bumping each other and laughing at everything. How good to feel happy and silly! They carried the glass balls they still had. As they walked home, carriages of sightseers bought souvenirs from them.

"How much did we make?" Hallelujah asked. They stopped in the middle of the street. Daniel held the cigar box while Maura counted. Her eyes grew wide.

"What's wrong?" Elizabeth asked.

"Must've made a mistake." She counted again. "Sixty-six dollars," she reported in a whisper. She had never seen so much money.

"That's eleven dollars apiece," said Hallelujah, matter-of-factly. "Not bad for one day's work!"

"I got two dollars more," Patrick said.

Elizabeth said, "I don't have enough for my souvenirs."

"Here," Hallelujah said. "Take your souvenirs and take your money, too. We're all partners. Anyone else want some?"

"I got a pretty one," Daniel said reaching.

"This has been fun," said Maura. "And tomorrow we can sell more."

"More and more and more," Hallelujah called. "Look, a rich people's carriage!" She darted over with several glass balls in her hand. The man bought three souvenirs for three dollars.

Elizabeth glanced after her, then lowered her face. She tucked her yellow hair under her bonnet, and stood with bonnet pulled forward and face down until the carriage rolled past.

"Hurry," she called catching up. "Give me my money."

They divided the money, eleven dollars apiece. The last three dollars they left in the cigar box to make change for the next day.

As they neared Twelfth and State, Patrick asked: "Do we have to give *them* all our money?"

"It's our business," Hallelujah said. She remembered Mary Jane. It must have hurt for her sister to hand over all her pay to Mr. Joseph week after week. And to think that Hallelujah had threatened to tattle that Mary Jane had kept fifty cents for herself! Hallelujah felt terrible about it now.

"We could give some and keep some," Maura said.

"Hurray!" called Rheba. "I'se for keeping some."

"Halves?" Maura asked.

"Let's say we keep six and give them five?" said Patrick.

"Sounds good to me," Hallelujah said, thinking of how nice it would be to have her own money. "Now that's a secret. Nobody tell, all right?"

Outside the kitchen door Elizabeth began scrubbing her face furiously. "Find my dress," she called to Hallelujah.

"Your dress?" asked Hallelujah. "Miss Tilly hasn't washed

this week. Monday was wash day, but she was too busy."

"That's all right," said Elizabeth. "I'll wear it like that."

"Why? You can keep wearing my dress."

Elizabeth raised her face and smiled happily. "Oh, do you know what? Those people in the carriage who bought the last glass balls from you?"

"Yes."

"They were my mama and papa and two little brothers and my cousin, Emily. I'm sure they're looking for me. They'll be here soon."

Hallelujah's mouth hung open. "Why didn't you run to them?"

"Oh, I couldn't let them see me with . . . with . . ."

"With what?"

"Well, my mama and papa wouldn't have been glad to see me."

"They wouldn't have been glad to see you?"

"Get my dress. You don't understand. You see, my parents don't associate with . . . with . . . people they consider lower class people. I'm sure they would rather me dead than running the streets with Irish and coloreds."

Mouth open, Hallelujah shook her head from side to side. "I can't believe it. You saw your mama, your real mama, and you couldn't run and hug her?"

"Where's my dress? Quick."

"That's crazy!" Hallelujah said, hands on hips.

"My blue taffeta dress!"

"Get it yourself, it's still in the barn. I'm not your servant. Change out there, but hurry, I'm hungry. Miss Tilly won't let me eat until you come," and she added bitterly, "I have to be polite to my rich guest!"

"Be nice to me, Hallelujah, it's not my fault I'm rich!"
Train whistles blew, one after another.

The soup pots were never both full, and never both
empty. Ladles of meat and potatoes and carrots and cabbage
constantly emptied one pot. And smothered chunks of salt-
pork meat and potatoes and carrots and shredded cabbage
constantly refilled another. After a day of selling souvenirs,
Hallelujah thought the soup was the most delicious food in
the world.

Miss Tilly had baked wheat rolls to go with the bowl of
soup. They buttered the rolls until they dripped.

Elizabeth sat straight every time a carriage rolled past.

Hallelujah watched her in wonderment. Would Elizabeth keep her promise to God to be kind toward all people?

Miss Tilly and Mr. Joseph and Mr. Post didn't ask why
Elizabeth was wearing her scorched smelly blue taffeta dress.
Perhaps they could guess, Hallelujah thought.

After supper in the dining room Hallelujah put six
dollars and a glass ball on the table for Mr. Joseph. She
kept five dollars for herself. At the same time she gave
a colorful glass ball to Edward Joseph, and one to Mary
Jane.

Miss Tilly served tea in her shined-up silver teapot. The
lilies were beautiful on the sides. "Gonna use it and enjoy
it," she said. "It wasn't even stained inside. Bet that other
lady didn't even enjoy her silver teapot."

When Mr. Joseph saw money on the table, he frowned.
"What's this? How did you earn money?" He seemed jeal-
ous.

Hallelujah said softly, "We sold the glass balls as souvenirs of the fire. People paid a dollar apiece for them."

Mr. Post cleared his throat. "Now that's right smart of the children. I passed their souvenir stand several times. They making money while they're out of school. And, good thing too, 'cause we men don't get paid till the end of the week."

Edward Joseph wasn't to be outdone. He reached in his pocket and pulled out money, too. He spread twelve dollars on the table. "I made this painting signs."

Hallelujah wondered how much he really made.

"Thank the good Lord," Miss Tilly said. "Our pantry is real low. We need flour, lard, milk, butter."

Mr. Joseph brushed the money into his big rough hands. "At this rate I can buy my machines. I can set up in business again sooner than I thought."

"Food first," said Miss Tilly firmly. She pulled part of the money back from him.

Mary Jane stared at a candle through her red, green, and blue glass ball. "This is so beautiful!"

A carriage clip-clopped on the street. Elizabeth sat forward. When it didn't stop, she slid back in the cane bottom chair.

Mr. Post noticed her. He pulled a single-sheet newspaper from his coat pocket. "Your name's here," he said. "And here your mama and papa are asking about you."

He read aloud: "Mr. Farwell seeks little girl, white hair, blue eyes, twelve years old in blue taffeta dress."

He shook the newspaper. "Only half a sheet, and the *Evening Journal Extra* sold out in an hour. Newsboys couldn't believe it!"

*   *   *

That night the girls slept in the room with Mary Jane. The Polish family had moved in with friends beyond the fire in the West Division. Mary Jane slept in a high bed with headboard and footboard of carved maple. She kept her journal and stories hidden under her mattress. On the bedside table sat her ink bottle, wooden pens, and pen points.

The little girls slept in a bed pulled from under the big one. It was called a trundle bed, and was little more than a mattress on a box with rollers.

"This is nice and soft," Elizabeth said. "Not as soft as my feather bed, but after the hay . . ."

"I know," said Hallelujah. "I don't miss the rats and owls. But I kinda liked the fresh smell of hay. Up here it smells smoky."

"That's my dress," Elizabeth said.

Mary Jane told her, "Put it in the hall, quick!"

As she returned, Elizabeth said, "Tomorrow they'll find me."

Hallelujah climbed between the covers, and shook her head. "I'll never understand people hating other people that much."

At three o'clock in the morning Hallelujah woke up. Her ruffled white curtains were blowing at the window. The wind was stronger. She tiptoed to shut the window and peered into the street.

Gaslights not burning. The lamplighter was out of his job, but it was still bright outside. Fires reflected off a cloudy sky. Coal yards, grain elevators, lumberyards, and spilled oil still burned and lit the night sky.

This was Wednesday, October 11, 1871.

As she returned to bed, she heard a pelting sound. A clatter on the roof. Her first thought was of firebrands. Would their roof catch on fire?

Had the fire changed direction? Were they no longer safe?

Chapter Sixteen

IN HER BED IN THE FRONT ROOM MISS TILLY moaned in her sleep. The pelting sounds had disturbed her, too.

Elizabeth sat up. "Is it fire?"

Mary Jane threw off her coverlet.

Hallelujah ran to the window, jerked back the curtains, and stuck out her head. Face staring at the sky, she laughed aloud. "No, rain! Come see." She held her arm out to feel the wetness.

Mary Jane knelt smiling beside her.

"Rain," Hallelujah shouted. "Now the fires will go out!"

From the front bedroom Miss Tilly called, "Thank the good Lord!"

"Amen to that," called Mr. Joseph.

"Amen!" Mr. Post added.

Hallelujah heard the Sullivan children next door. She stared out her window. Their faces were pressed to the glass. "Rain!" she called.

Raising their windows, they called back, "Rain! St. Patrick helped us, rain!" They cheered and laughed.

Elizabeth stood at the window beside Mary Jane. "It really is rain," she said softly. "Rain!"

As she closed the window, Hallelujah said, "I don't think I've ever been so glad to see rain."

"Nor me," said Elizabeth. The two girls returned to bed.

Mary Jane sat on the floor to write in her journal.

The next morning Miss Tilly carried kettles of hot water to the barn for Elizabeth to have a warm bath. Elizabeth bathed in a galvanized tub while Hallelujah guarded the barn door.

The sky Hallelujah gazed at was filled with lavender-blue rain clouds. From time to time raindrops splattered noisily on dry leaves. The air smelled somewhat clean and fresh for the first time in months.

On the straw, Miss Tilly laid Elizabeth's underwear, petticoats, dress, and bonnet. During the early morning hours she had washed the clothes and ironed them dry enough to wear. In spite of cinder holes, Elizabeth looked elegant again.

Hallelujah had forgotten how pretty her clothes had been.

When they trotted into the barn, the Sullivan children stared at Elizabeth and backed away.

Daniel asked, "You mean you're gonna sell souvenirs looking like that?"

Elizabeth said, "Oh, no. Not today. I'm waiting for my papa to come for me."

Train whistles sounding louder in wet weather, continued to blow at their stations.

Hallelujah shook her head and led Elizabeth into the kitchen. Somehow the sight of her friend dressed in finery bothered her. Maybe they weren't equal after all.

Both girls were silent during breakfast. Elizabeth looked at Hallelujah and tried to speak, but couldn't. Hallelujah glanced at her from time to time, then lowered her eyes angrily. They had almost been friends, but that was when they both wore unbleached cotton dresses.

For breakfast they ate boiled codfish, slab bacon, corn bread cut in squares in a warming basket, and fried eggs. The eggs were piled slippery high on a huge platter.

Elizabeth cleared her throat. "Aren't those a lot of eggs?"

"Wait," Hallelujah said, sipping her milk.

Within minutes the mountain of eggs was gone, and so was the basketful of corn bread. Visiting church friends and strangers, who were working together, helped themselves.

Miss Tilly took off her apron. She pulled on her bonnet and tossed a shawl around her shoulders.

"I be going to market," she said. "Cooked the last food in the house." A soft woven basket was over her arm. "Mr. Joseph don't get paid till end of the week. You children's money will pay for food!"

Hallelujah's heart seemed to waltz in three step. She held her breath and squeezed her arms against her sides. Her money was paying for food for her family to eat. And not only for them, but for hungry strangers from the fire!

And to think, she was just a child. How proud she felt!

Just then there was impatient pounding on the front door. She ran to answer as Miss Tilly stood frowning in the kitchen doorway. Most friends came in the back door.

A handsome black carriage with green fringe and two bay horses waited in the street. A red-faced servant had knocked. He held a copy of the *Chicago Tribune* in his hand.

He frowned at Hallelujah. "May I speak to the lady of the house?"

She called for Miss Tilly and ran back to the kitchen.

From there Hallelujah could hear him ask, "Is there a child named Elizabeth Farwell here?"

"I believes so," Miss Tilly answered softly.

Elizabeth heard them too and turned to Hallelujah who stood by her side. Frantically, Elizabeth grabbed for her hand. "Don't let it make a difference. Please. Can't we be sisters?"

Hallelujah backed away. "I don't know." She shook her head. "You are upper class, and I forgot. I wonder if you'll even speak to me on the street."

"Of course!" Elizabeth cried. She stamped her foot. "I will, I will, but you have to speak, too. We're always free to be ourselves. Aren't we?"

"Not if folks around us tell us how to think," said Hallelujah.

"But we know better. Isn't that what we learned from the fire? The burned homes. The dead bodies. People are all equal: we all suffer, we all laugh, we all bleed red." Tears brimmed Elizabeth's eyes. "Didn't you say that? Aren't you the one who taught me that we're all equally special?"

"I suppose so." Hallelujah was crying, too.

"Oh, Hallelujah, I'm afraid."

"Afraid of your papa and mama?"

"No. Afraid of me. I want to know about people. You taught me that everybody is somebody. For three days I worked, I helped people. I never want to forget this. Am I so young I'll forget?" She covered her mouth with her hand. Sobbing, she said, "Will it be like it was before? Precious little Elizabeth who can't be dirtied by common people?"

Suddenly, Hallelujah hugged her. "No, remember? You promised God! You won't forget. We're old enough. And clothes and your parents can't make you a snob if you don't want to be."

Miss Tilly called, "Miss Elizabeth?"

Elizabeth said, "Promise you won't be snobbish either. Promise." Her face was awash with tears.

Hallelujah hugged her. They held each other tightly. "I won't be mean. I promised God, too."

"Promise we'll always be sisters!"

"Always!"

"If we say so, we can," Elizabeth said.

"We are sisters. We shared the Great Chicago Fire, we shared a barn, we shared a bed and food."

Elizabeth said, "No one can take that away from us."

"No, they can't. Not even your parents. And now," said Hallelujah, reaching for a linen towel, "wipe your face before they think we've been beating you."

Elizabeth laughed and wiped her eyes. She and Hallelujah hugged again. Then she turned swiftly and ran to the front door and out. When she reached the carriage, the door opened briefly, an arm pulled her in. The door slammed shut, and the driver whipped the horses off at a rapid trot. Hallelujah and Miss Tilly stood in the doorway staring after them.

"So," said Miss Tilly slowly, "that's they thanks. Some rich folks ain't got the manners of a roach."

She could see that Hallelujah had been crying, and she rested her arm on Hallelujah's shoulders. "Never you mind, honey child," she said. "She didn't be like us."

Hallelujah thought, But she was! Already someone is changing my thinking. I have to hold fast. We *are* the same!

All morning Hallelujah and the Sullivans sold their souvenirs under rainy skies until they were wet to the skin. Their clothes clung like ivy vines, and their shoes slushed with each step, but they were happy. They were making money to help their families.

When they reached forty dollars, Hallelujah said, "Give me ten dollars. I'm cold and hungry."

"Working men don't quit," said Patrick.

"Working children can," Daniel said.

Just then they heard clapping. All the working people were clapping and pointing to soldiers in the distance wearing blue uniforms. The soldiers had knapsacks on their backs and muskets in their hands as they marched down the street. They arrived the morning of October 11, 1871.

The soldiers stared straight ahead as they swung their arms smartly. The wind blew locks of brown or yellow hair around their shoulders. Their cap visors were pulled low on their foreheads. To Hallelujah they looked like English and Irish men. Since the war, colored men weren't allowed in the army anymore.

A gentleman on horseback told the staring children: "Them's Sheridan's boys. Now we'll have some law and order in this here city."

Sheridan's "boys" looked more like grown men to Hal-

lelujah. She had heard that Governor Palmer sent for the
Fifth U.S. Infantry from Fort Leavenworth. The soldiers
wore blue uniforms with shiny brass buttons.

Breaking the formation of march, they immediately
began to clear a few city blocks to set up tents. Hallelujah
stared at them.

As she wandered home with her friends, there was a
fresh shower. Smoking rubble hissed in the rain. The damp
and the cold made her shiver and she felt lonesome. Elizabeth had been a friend, almost like a sister her age for a
while.

The Sullivan children were never able to talk about the
things she and Elizabeth had talked about. Maura would
look at her as if she were crazy. Mary Jane was too old.
Hallelujah's colored friends were still angry and full of hate
toward white people. Rheba understood a little, but Rheba
was shy. As a little slave child, she had been beaten, and
she had never recovered her faith in people.

Rachael from the West Division hadn't believed her
either. But Elizabeth had understood. They could talk about
the important things in life: who they were, what life was
all about.

Tears mingled with rain drops to roll down Hallelujah's
brown cheeks.

At the house Hallelujah heard Mr. Thomas Baker's voice
from the kitchen. The men were home for dinner at noon.
She felt hungry, but eating alone again after Elizabeth's
company wouldn't be much fun.

She ran around the house to the barn. Out there she
washed up in a tin pan filled with water, and changed into

dry clothes. The hay was pressed down where she and Elizabeth had made their bed.

White Star whinnied, and she patted his nose. She
felt better after rubbing his shiny warm coat. He seemed
to sense that she felt lonesome, and he nuzzled her
cheek.

Chapter Seventeen

WHEN HALLELUJAH OPENED THE KITCHEN door, everyone stopped talking and smiled at her. She stood still wondering, what now? "Miss Hallelujah," began Mr. Thomas Baker, "I just be telling your folks what a brave child you was."

Head still, she rolled her eyes to see everyone. Miss Tilly pressed a handkerchief to her eyes.

"I was brave?" Hallelujah asked.

"And saved our great city of Chicago!"

"Saved the city?"

Mr. Baker said: "This child stood in freezing lake waters with fire hailing all around her. And she stood there three hours holding a sack of millions of dollars."

Mr. Post was grinning. "Mr. LaSalle and me was wondering where you bank people got it. Thought maybe it came from New York on a train. But there wasn't much time to telegraph. . . ."

Millions of what? Hallelujah stepped forward and closed the door. Freezing water? No. She never got her shoes wet, the shoes she lost to a thief. Fire hailing? Yes. But it was hailing on everybody. And was it really three hours? From maybe four o'clock in the morning. And the man said it was seven o'clock when the sun rose. Three hours!

Millions? She opened her mouth and shut it. Never mind, she need not tell them she didn't know what she was holding. But, she should have guessed it was money! He worked for a bank.

"Mr. Baker," she said softly, "I was doing you a favor." Maybe now she could tell them what that had meant. How she appreciated what they had done for her and for her mother. "Mary Jane and Edward Joseph told me about how you helped my mama who's dead. How mama took us to the church. How you and the church people found us somewhere to live.

"How Miss Tilly and Mr. Joseph took us in with them. And Miss Tilly nursed my mama until she died. And now they're raising me like I was their own child. I remembered that. You asked me for a favor, and I did it. There was nothing else I could do."

Miss Tilly sat in her rocker by the stove and blew her nose.

Mr. Baker cleared his throat. Hallelujah hoped he wouldn't cry. She hated when men cried.

He said, "And you should have seen. She wrapped that money sack in a blanket. Fought off fire, so's our city could rise again."

He pointed to the Sullivan house. "You knows Patrick Sullivan's job? Well, Cyrus McCormick's ordered five buildings. His reaper factory on the river burned, but he's building five more. Our banks got his money to pay for it."

He waved his arm. "Not only that, folks be telling me 'twas your Hallelujah what saved a congregation in a church. Opened the doors and called, 'Fire!' Five minutes after the last person got out, the church was in flames. And ten minutes after that, it be all gone. Burned clear to the ground."

Mr. Joseph cleared his throat. "I always thought she might come to some good end," he said.

Hallelujah felt pleased with herself. No one was saying that she was a pitiful little orphan now!

A train whistle blew and she remembered yearning for adventure. Well, she had known enough adventure to last a long time.

Two months later Hallelujah was glad to attend school again. It was held in a dark choir loft until a new school could be built. She learned that seven children from their school had burned to death in the fire. Other families, too: Schumachers, Smiths, Petersons, Noblickis, Meullers, Zielinskis, Taliankos, Browns, and Szymanowskis.

Her classmate Jay Sky had died in the fire saving a Swedish mother and her children. He got the children out, but a burning wall fell on him. It must have been shortly after he talked to her at the fire.

Hallelujah couldn't help feeling that she might have been the last friend he spoke to before dying to save strangers. He was dead, her Indian classmate. Although white people despised Indians, he gave his life saving a white mother and children. Hallelujah's heart ached over Jay Sky's death. She hardly knew him, but she always felt close to him because of how some white people treated people of color.

*   *   *

The city grew. At first the homeless stayed in schools, churches, warehouses, or with other families. Later, a tent city gave shelter; then wooden barracks were built for the winter. As people earned money, they ordered homes built for themselves. Everywhere fine homes were being built that winter, thousands of homes.

Coal yards and grain elevators still burned. The smell of smoke filled the air constantly. However, buildings sprang up on every street. Each city block had several buildings rising.

It was said over ten thousand commercial buildings were rising from the ashes. Overnight everyone was a carpenter or a mortar maker or a brick mason. There was work for everyone.

One evening Mr. Joseph said it in an interesting way. He said: "Chicago was lowered by fire, and Chicago's rising by fire."

Hallelujah asked, "How?"

"Fire's keeping the mortar warm enough to use and the men warm enough to use it."

Miss Tilly put biscuits on the dining room table to go with pork chops and potatoes and cabbage. There were sweet potato pies for dessert.

"Thank the Lord it be a mild winter," said Miss Tilly. "Not like them winters of sixty-nine and seventy. And no one's out of work or hungry."

No, Hallelujah thought. No longer did she hug the heavy pot of food against her tan cotton dress. No longer did the Sullivan children hide from her as she brought the good smelling food to keep them from starving. No longer did the parents sneak to return the empty pot in shame, unable to even thank their neighbors out of embarrassment. Now everyone had work and money. And no one was hungry. Hallelujah was happy about that!

She heard footsteps on the porch and someone pounded on the front door. Since it was after dark, Mr. Joseph went to the door. But Hallelujah's curiosity drove her to tiptoe behind him.

In the doorway Elizabeth stood beside her driver. She was dressed in an outfit of gold-colored velvet with a white fur muff. Hallelujah squealed and ran to hug her.

Elizabeth rushed to her, and they embraced tightly. Both of them were crying and laughing at the same time.

Hallelujah said, "Your sachet scent is better than the smoke you used to smell like."

"And you've got cabbage on your breath. It smells delicious. I ate the nicest meals of my life here."

"Better not let you mama hear that," Hallelujah said.

"Oh, she wouldn't mind. She knows how terrible our cook is, but I'm nice to him just the same!"

They both hugged and giggled and hugged again. Hallelujah was pleased to hear that Elizabeth was keeping her promise. Elizabeth turned to her driver who was carrying boxes, and pointed, "I have some things for you. Quick, open the boxes."

There were three large boxes. Tearing the wrapping off the top box, Hallelujah found a green velvet bonnet with satin ribbons.

"Try it on. Right away."

Hallelujah fitted it carefully over her six braids.

"There, I knew you'd look beautiful in green," Elizabeth said. "Now the next box."

Hallelujah reached for the smallest one, but Elizabeth snatched that one away. "No, that one."

Sighing loudly but with a grin, Hallelujah put her hands on her hips. "You sure know how to boss people around."

"Well, I've got a reason."

The largest box held a beautiful green velvet dress to match the bonnet. Shaking the heavy velvet folds, Hallelujah twisted back and forth with it in front of her.

"Thank you, Elizabeth. These are so fine. I'll wear them for church on Christmas Day. They're so pretty!"

"Now, this!" And Elizabeth pranced up and down. She held the smallest box out to her.

The box was the size of a shoe box, or a box for boots. Hallelujah wondered how Elizabeth knew her size, and if the shoes would match her dress and bonnet. She removed the ribbons carefully to save for her braids.

Peeling the tissue paper back, she saw a doll with brown hair and brown eyes. The doll had a smiling white face painted on a china head, and brown shoes painted on china feet.

"Oh," she called. "A china-face doll!"

"It's called porcelain, but it's like china. Do you like it?" asked Elizabeth.

The doll was dressed in an outfit to match Hallelujah's new green velvet. The doll's dress was the same material and style; the doll's bonnet was the same green velvet. Even the ribbons matched.

Elizabeth put her head to the side. "Do you think Suzy will like her even if she's not colored? I couldn't find a colored doll, but this doll has brown hair and eyes."

Hallelujah laughed aloud. "I was just thinking about that. I'll have to explain to Suzy how all dolls are equally special."

As they hugged, carriage bells outside rang impatiently. Elizabeth ran into the dining room and hugged Miss Tilly. She shook hands with Mr. Joseph, Mr. Post, and Edward Joseph. She hugged Mary Jane.

"Thank you for good food and somewhere to stay when I was lost. My mama and papa had been worried. They were glad I was comfortable." The bells rang again, and Elizabeth ran out to her carriage waving her hand behind her.

On the front porch Hallelujah stood in her new bonnet holding the china-face doll. She watched Elizabeth climb up the carriage steps.

Elizabeth stood on the top carriage step and called: "Will you name her Elizabeth or Betsy after me?"

"Oh, no," Hallelujah called. "You had a Betsy doll in the fire. I would never name her Elizabeth."

"Then what will you name her?" A lady's arm tried to yank her into the carriage. At a command, the driver started the carriage to roll, the horses pulled it forward.

Elizabeth clung to the doorway. "What will you name her?"

Hallelujah knew the name. For a long time she had known what she would name a doll, if she ever had a second doll.

Hallelujah was no longer a morning child with the heaviness of evening in her heart. Now she was a morning child with sunrise in her heart.

"What will you name her?"

Hallelujah raised both arms high, holding the new doll in one hand.

Loudly she called, "Hope!"

Author's Note

IN THIS STORY OF CHILDREN LIVING DURING THE Great Chicago Fire of 1871, the events are all true, but the characters are fictional. I learned about what happened from letters, diaries, and articles written by people who were in the fire and who walked those same Chicago streets.

The planing mill fire had made the firemen exhausted, but no fire fighters could have stopped the flames on a night with wind like that. The fire began in a small barn behind Patrick O'Leary's cottage at 137 DeKoven Street. Whether or not the legendary cow kicked over a lantern is unknown.

The galelike winds and superheated air from the fire made masses of hurling flames which lifted objects such as hay and doors and blew them for distances to start new fires. The fire raged for the three days of October 8, 9, and 10 in 1871, burning a section of Chicago that was four and a half miles long and about a mile wide. Rain on the early morning of October 11 stopped the fire.

Of the total Chicago populaton of 334,000 at the time of the fire, 3,000 were black like Hallelujah. Many of them had escaped slavery on the Underground Railroad. Others had been born free in Illinois.

In the fire, about 300 people were burned to death, and about 100,000 were left without homes, a third of the population. However, before the fire stopped, people were hauling ashes and readying bricks to rebuild. A "colored" man, name unknown, helped save cash from a bank to rebuild the city.

With as many as 10,000 buildings in construction at a time, Chicago was rebuilt in three years. By 1893, when a rebuilt Chicago hosted the World's Fair, the population had grown to two million.

Children in all times need to realize how important their lives are. Children piled bricks, hauled ash, and sold souvenirs to help their families and their city. The fire taught them as it should teach us, that diversity of color, class, and culture should add interest to life but should never be allowed to divide us.

We are all equally children of God and of our universe.

Bibliography

Angle, Paul M. *The Great Chicago Fire*. Chicago: Chicago Historical Society, 1971.

Civil War Diary of James T. Ayers. Edited by John Hope Franklin. Chicago: Illinois State Historical Society, 1947.

Cook, May Estelle. *Little Old Oak Park*. Oak Park, Ill.: Privately printed, 1961.

Historic City: The Settlement of Chicago. Chicago: Department of Development and Planning, 1976. Includes maps.

Knudtson, Thomas. *Chicago: The Rising City*. Chicago: Chicago Publishing Company, 1975.

Kogan, Herman, and Lloyd Wendt. *Chicago, A Pictorial History*. New York: E. P. Dutton and Co., 1958.

Lowe, David. *The Great Chicago Fire*. New York: Dover Publications, 1979.

Mayer, Harold M., and Richard C. Wade. *Chicago, Growth of a Metropolis*. Chicago: University of Chicago Press, 1969.